The SOUND *of* HOOVES

BRYAN MACMAHON

POOLBEG

To
Augustine Martin

Published in 1985 by
The Bodley Head Ltd
Paperback edition 1995 by
Poolbeg Press Ltd,
Knocksedan House,
123 Baldoyle Industrial Estate,
Dublin 13, Ireland

© Bryan MacMahon 1985

The moral right of the author has been asserted.

A catalogue record for this book is available from the British Library.

ISBN 1 85371 466 6

Cover photograph by Mike O'Toole
Cover design by Poolbeg Group Services Ltd
Printed by The Guernsey Press Ltd,
Vale, Guernsey, Channel Islands.

Contents

Some of these stories first appeared in the *Irish Press*, *The Best Irish Short Stories*, *Winter's Tales from Ireland*, *Aquarius* and *The End of the World*.

The Sound of Hooves

Everyone in the town said that the old harnessmaker was failing. For one thing he was now far slower when raising his head from his work to listen to the sound of hooves.

When it was gently put to him that since he lived alone he'd be better off in the old people's home he said he'd chance another winter on his own floor. And when even the priest asked, 'What have you here, Shaun, that you won't have in the home?' the old man answered firmly but courteously, 'My independence, Father!'

So people left it at that. They shook their heads of course, said he'd fall into the open fire and be burned alive, argued whether he was eighty-nine or ninety-four and went off about their business. In matters like these one can go so far and no farther.

So, faltering and tottering, the old harnessmaker continued to occupy the perch—for perch it was since his stool was precariously balanced on a heap of old harness—he had occupied for over eighty years. This, ever since the day when as a barefooted boy he had run home from school at luncheon time to be met by his whitefaced mother who said, 'You're not going back to school again, Shaun. Your father caught his hand in the hairbeating machine and he'll work no more. Go out and take the shop as best you can.'

Now, at last, judging by his pallor and his trembling movements, it seemed as if the old tradesman would literally die in harness.

*　*　*

The country town was quiet as the clerical student walked down the long main street. It was the afternoon of the weekly half-holiday on a day in August. Most of the townspeople had gone off to the seaside. The clerical student liked to have the town like that. He needed quietness to reflect. He had only a few weeks in which to come to a decision. He had left the ecclesiastical college the previous Easter on the understanding that he would think matters over before his ordination.

The young man was dressed in black trousers under a dark green windcheater with a brown shirt and tie. His face was pale, the skin rather translucent. His long fingers were delicate. His eyes were dark brown. His forehead was high and slightly protuberant.

Half-way down the street, having passed the jeweller's and the boutique, he turned into the harnessmaker's shop. There he sat down on the red form that ran parallel to the time-eaten counter. He rested his shoulder-blades against the oats bin and looked up at the harnessmaker. The tradesman was intent on his work.

Neither spoke for an appreciable time.

At last the old fellow raised his head. 'Is this you?' he said.

'Yes,' very quietly. Then, as if pondering some problem, the old man ceased working and turned his face so that his features took the window light.

To himself the clerical student said, 'People say that he will soon be dead. He has often spoken to me of horses: he has never mentioned human love.'

The student looked about him as if seeing things for the first time.

There were blackened hooks in the ceiling from which depended breechings, bridles and half-finished horse collars together with donkeys' winkers and plaited reins. Across the lightweight panes of the mullioned windows were stair-rods through which were threaded dog muzzles and bridle bits, buckles and harness brasses.

These articles, though seemingly offered for sale, were not for sale at all. 'If I part with them, I'll have nothing to sell,' was the smiling reply of the old man to a prospective customer.

'He never tires of speaking to me of horses,' the clerical student told himself again. 'Show horses, stepping horses, thoroughbreds, work-horses, Connemara and pit ponies. Now that perhaps he is nearing his end he may speak to me of human love.'

The leather gripped in the clam between his thighs, the old man resumed his slow stitching. Driving the awl through layers of leather he crouched a little, gathered himself around the shoulders, then with a tiny grunt of exertion drove deeply until the point of the awl gleamed through on the other side. Gathered thus, his shoulders, misshapen almost as a result of the many years of his trade, indicated the waning of a great strength. Then, the awl-blade withdrawn, having inserted one needle bearing the waxed thread on one side of the hole and another similar needle on the other side, he drew the stitches tight by spreading his arms like wings.

I need to be spoken to regarding matters other than theology and philosophy, the clerical student told himself. Just now, I am what is locally called 'nervy'. The calves of my legs tremble when I wake at morning. This is an indirect result of my inability to reach a decision. But first I have to clarify certain issues. Here is an old fellow who appears to have voluntarily accepted celibacy. Has he ever been tempted as I am constantly being tempted? In terms of the animal world he has always been close to the elemental rhythm of mating, birth and death. He is one of the few people to whom I have access. Does he possess the knowledge I need? I do not even know what I am looking for. Yet, I feel that I will recognize and appreciate it when I find it.

Women are at the core of my problem, the student told himself. I fear the lonely stretching forward of priestly life until it peters out into eccentricity and death. And after death—the judgement! And yet this old fellow has never married. Nor has he ever spoken of love.

There was little sound in the old shop except the rustle of wings from the goldfinch's cage in the fanlight, the footstep of a desultory pedestrian on the pavement outside, the sniff of a dog at the doorpost.

'Very well!' The old man had raised his head slowly, painfully almost. He paused for effect, then began as if continuing a conversation he had broken off days before. 'The first three Arab stallions in Ireland were Byerley Turk, Darley Arabian and Godolphin Barb.' A long pause. 'Byerley Turk was a British Army horse: it could be that he fought at the Battle of the Boyne. He was at stud in Ireland for a while then. When he went back to England he got wonder horses off mares selected from the Royal stables.'

Silence as the old man resumed his work. The student began to ponder the pattern of the harness brasses: plumes, foxheads, serpents, brandished swords, a plough team, carriages, horseshoes and chanticleers. He began to analyse the smells in the air about him: wax, old man, rye straw, dung-soiled harness, leather oils, chafed timber and cardboard advertisements.

'Did you ever hear tell of Colonel Hall Walker from Tullig Stud in Kildare?' the old man asked.

'No!'

'He mated stallions and mares by astrology.' The old fellow cackled and squeezed a drop from the tip of his nose. 'Unless the signs of the Zodiac were right, he refused service. I think he had stallions called Blandford and Big Game. In a thoroughbred mating the mare is decked or tied. For fear she'd come to harm.'

'I see.'

Silence again. The old clock on the wall just inside the window ticked on. Below the clock-face the pendulum showed fitfully as it swung behind a small glass panel.

The young man half rose from the stool and took a lump of wax from the counter. The wax was black and brown in colour. Falling back on his seat he put the wax to his nostrils, then began to knead it between his fingers. The wax was soft; that meant that the weather would remain fine. Old Shaun had taught him that wax was a barometer of sorts.

As his fingers worked, the student looked up at the old thin face above him. The poised skull, its bone structure winning through, the cropped grey-green scalp, the cyanosed lips, the shrivelled dewlap of the throat, the brown wens on the cheek, the bright speedwell-coloured eyes all indicated that the old man had not long to live.

Suddenly the old man's head was alert. To what is he listening? the young man asked himself. To the twitter and rustle of the goldfinch? To the tick-tock of the clock?

The student's ears caught the faint clop of horses' hooves.

Listening acutely, the harnessmaker's jaw fell. A web of spittle joined his upper lip to his lower. He drove the awl deep, whisked it out, inserted one needle, then the other. The drawn stitches squeaked faintly as they were snapped home. The sound of hooves drew closer. The saddler ceased to work. His eyes were fixed on the sunlit roadway outside. Catching his nose between thumb and forefinger he squeezed the drop from his nostrils.

Both knew exactly what was coming: a pseudo-gipsy caravan in which the French young take their Irish holidays.

* * *

Walking purposefully in midroad in front of the vehicle a young woman appears. She is dressed in faded reds and blues. She is looking up at the painted shopfronts on either side of the street. Drawn by a lazy horse the caravan follows close behind. A second young woman, the reins slack in her hands, is sitting on the small seat at one side of the caravan doorway. The leading young woman spies the saddler's shop. As she turns her head there is a chatter of excited talk in French. A sleep-tousled young man appears in the doorway of the vehicle. A second young man, who was walking in midroad behind the caravan, comes up to join the others. The little procession comes to a halt in midroad.

There is a short council of war. All four are looking at the harnessmaker's shop. The old man inside can see the newcomers through the grimy glass of the window, yet by a trick of the light they cannot see him.

A decision is reached. One of the two men leads the horse towards a pole on the other side of the roadway and stands there holding the reins. The other man, seen emerging from the caravan, is clutching a basket. Leaping to the ground, he indicates that he is setting off in search of a shop. Both the young women approach the harnessmaker's.

The student gazes steadily at the old boards of the counter in front of him. The harnessmaker has resumed his stitching: his fingers seem livelier than before.

The two women stand at the shop window and peer in. The younger of the two ventures to move directly in front of the doorway. There she is spotlighted by the afternoon sun. Raising his head the old man pretends that he has just now discovered her. He straightens up from his work and smiles. He has only a few yellow teeth.

The second woman joins the first. Together they enter the shop. Their eyes take in every detail. They examine the old glass case at the back of the shop in which the figure of the craftsman is barely reflected, the passepartout-framed pictures of old-time race-horses, the yellowed posters proclaiming the potency of stallions, the half finished articles of harness. One of the young women turns to look up at the goldfinch in its cage then glances down at the student.

Gesticulation. A few sentences in French. The harnessmaker looks at the student. The student lowers his head as if to convey that he does not wish to be involved. One of the young women gestures about her own neck to indicate to Shaun that the strap of the bridle is broken. Would he please mend it?

The old man leans forward to spy out the mare by the pole on the opposite side of the street: using his awl as a pointer he says, 'Bring it hether to me!' He speaks rather loudly as if addressing a deaf person. The smaller of the two women hurries off and returns with the bridle.

The saddler allows the bridle to dangle from his hand. 'The throatlatch is broken,' he says pointing out the break with the point of his awl.

The woman tries to repeat the word 'throatlatch' after him.

With a smile the harnessmaker indicates to the pair that they should take a seat. Almost before the student realizes it, the young women have seated themselves, one on either side of him. He finds a flush mounting to his face.

Shaun examines the broken strap, places the rough edges together, bends part of the old strap so that it snaps abruptly, indicates that the leather is rotten and that he will have to cut a new throatlatch. The young women nod their agreement.

The student is tense. The young women remotely convey to each other that they recognize his tension. And that they are pleased by it. Looking over-studiedly before him the young man is conscious of the elemental smell of young women.

The ticking of the clock. The crack of a seed against the bars of the cage.

The old man slowly sharpens his knife. Placing the length of hide close to his chest and catching his knife as if he is about to stab underhand, he draws the blade towards him as he cuts the length of strap. This done, he unwinds on thumb and forefinger a figure-of-eight of waxed thread. He threads both needles, spins the needle on the wax end and with a glance of subdued pride at the three seated on the form he begins to stitch.

As he works, the old man's arms, recurrently extended, mimic the act of flying.

The smell of wax, ammonia, copperas, linseed, polish, leather oil and human sweat.

The student sees the awl in the old man's hand with new eyes. The little tool has a female head, a womanly waist and hips that fuse as they taper downward to an elongated leg. The tool as a whole resembles a ballerina on tiptoe. The comparison ends as he realizes that the blade of the awl is male. He watches closely as the blade penetrates the leather. Perhaps the tool in the old man's hand is both male and female, he reminds himself with a tremulous smile.

Cautiously the student unclenches his fist and ventures to glance down. Lying in his palm, modelled in wax, is the crude figure of a woman. Alert head, pronounced breasts and buttocks—there she is. Has he made this image consciously? He tightens his fist about the image but not before the young woman nearer the door has seen what lies in his palm. She conveys her discovery to the other woman—the student fails to apprehend the code or signal used—but he knows that the message has shuttled across his face. And that, almost instantaneously, an answer is being sent back.

A few moments of apparent inaction. Then the thigh of one of the young women touches his. The student holds his breath. As he inclines his head the minutest fraction towards her the other young woman's thigh touches his. This cannot be a coincidence! How can they be so intuitively aware of his predicament? Very slowly he releases his breath. Then his outer forearm is conscious of the touch of a pendent breast. Her alibi? She is leaning outwards to address her companion on some aspect of the old man's work. If the breast of the young woman to my right touches me . . . And even as he mentally forms the question that is what happens.

Monosyllables pass from woman to woman: the student under-stands French tolerably well, but the young women are using language beneath language.

The old man works on. The awl penetrates, the needles pry, the great wings of Icarus are spread. There is a sense of waiting.

The clam between the saddler's thighs clacks as the finished strap is released. The old man places the strap on the side of the clam and briskly rubs the stitches, leaning his weight on the haft of the knife. The young man tightens his fist about the wax figure in his palm until he is convinced that it is unrecognizable as the image of a woman. The girl nearest the door thrusts her hand down inside her sweater and brings up a string purse. She comes to her feet and, moving a step closer to the counter, indicates that she wishes to pay.

The harnessmaker smiles; then, his blue eyes growing brighter, he leans forward and says, 'Nothing at all, my girl!'

A series of ejaculations.

'Tell her she can pay me next year,' the old saddler tells the student.

The student says quietly, *'Le vieil homme dit que vous pourrez régler l'an prochain.'*

'Vraiment!' the woman says thoughtfully. She glances from the student to her companion, then back to the student.

'Tell her it is nothing,' the saddler insists.

'Il dit que ça n'a pas d'importance.'

'Merci.'

The young woman on the red stool comes to her feet. She takes a small square of pale mauve silk from the breast pocket of her blouse. Catching it by a corner she drops it loose. As she does so the smell of scent pervades the shop. She gathers the scrap of silk in her cupped fingers, tightens her grip on it and as the material releases itself she brings it to her nostrils. She inhales deeply, then places it under the saddler's nose. 'Hm?' she says archly.

The old man closes his eyes and inhales deeply.

'Aaah!' he says softly, as he releases his breath.

To the student. *'Et vous?'* The student inhales.

'C'est un souvenir!' the woman says brightly. She looks about her, then hangs the handkerchief on a corner of a picture of Bendigo the sire.

The young man who had gone shopping is standing at the sunlit doorway.

The women show him the mended bridle. They explain that the old man will not accept payment. There are renewed sounds of appreciation. With a final glance upward at the caged finch, and downward at the pale-faced student, all three move out of the shop and across the roadway.

The bridle rings. The caravan begins to lurch forward. The sound of hooves dies away.

Prickspur and snaffle, surcingle, martingale and side-saddle, cantle, pommel and flap, brasses, terrets, hoosen, elm-bridges of donkeys' straddles daubed farmer's blue, bit, bridle, crupper and throatlatch. Throatlatch—the student pauses in his harness litany to savour the word. And now there is the mauve kerchief impregnated with perfume. There it hangs draped gently over the edge of the picture of the stallion.

*   *   *

14

When the sound of hooves had died away the old man cast about on the clutter beneath him as if unsure what task to begin. After a while he set a strap in the jaws of the clam, then groped overhead for the needles and wax thread which he had looped over the curve of a half-made horse collar. Failing to find them, he drove the awl deep into the leather, looked out the window, glanced sidelong at the piece of silk, smiled, squeezed his nostrils, looked thoughtfully down at the student.

There was a long pause.

'Twice I was tempted by women,' the old man began. 'The first time was when I was nineteen years of age. I was a hardy lad then. I was tipping away by myself in the shop, sittin' right there. My father an' my younger brother, God rest them both, were inside at their dinner. A lovely bouncing country girl came in enquiring after some job of her father's. We commenced chattin'. She had every eye on the crossdoor to the kitchen—as if she was afraid the curtain on the glass panel would start twitchin'.

' "You passed back our way in your trap and stepping pony last Sunday about five o'clock," she said.

' "I did," I said for I knew where she lived, beyond Drake's Wood down by the shore.

' "Ye were greatly admired!" she said again.

'That remark pleased me. There was a pause between us then. Her eyes were serious.

' "I know someone who admired yourself," she said.

' "Who would that be?" I asked.

' "There's tellin' in that!"

' "Was it a man or a woman?"

' "A woman. A young woman. Would you meet her at the Wood Cross a mile to the west of our house next Sunday, say at four o'clock?"

' "It's quiet there at that time," she went on when I made no answer.

' "If she was as nice as you, I would," I said at last.

' "That's settled so."

' "Would it be any harm to ask her name?"

' "No harm at all. It's myself."

' "You're jokin'."

' "I'm in earnest."

'I took time to consider. She was a rich farmer's daughter. Good-lookin' too. There was big fortune coming to her. She could have her pick of many men. What business did she have with an apprentice harnessmaker, his hands cut to ribbons with work?

' "Very well," I said, "I'll be at the Wood Cross next Sunday evening at four o'clock!"

' "For sure?"

' "For sure!"

'Then we parted.'

The student waited. If he ran true to form the old fellow would now resume by referring to himself in the third person.

'Well, Shaun was at the Wood Cross in the pony and trap at four o'clock. He was there at five, six and seven. Still no trace of the bouncing young woman! Shaun hadn't slept much all that week with thinking of her, so at half-past seven he drove home like a madman, slashin' the pony till the animal was a lather of sweat.

' "That finishes me with women," I swore. "Never again will I trust one of them." A girl friend of hers came in a few days later with a note. No one here but myself. The note said that she was coming out the door when a married sister of hers landed in from Dublin. I found out later that that was a lie. I made a joke of it to the messenger but when she asked me if I'd be at the Cross the following Sunday instead, "I won't," I said, "nor Sunday month, nor Sunday twenty years." "You're a fool, Shaun," the girl said as she left the shop.

'The bouncing girl died twelve months ago. Her eldest son was a canon and he read over her coffin. I met the girl-messenger last June by accident at the Cattle Show here above. She was an old old woman. As I am an old old man. She brought me back well over sixty-five years when she lowered the window of her motor and croaked out my name. "Do you know the real reason why she didn't come?" she whispered as if it all had happened yesterday. "I don't," I said. "She was at the time of the month when a young woman doesn't want to meet a young man." Then I understood. "You're still a fool, Shaun!" she said as she rolled up the window of the car.'

I keep analysing silence, the student told himself, as if trying to break it down into its constituent elements.

'I was reared strict,' the old fellow went on as if talking to himself. 'I wasn't used to the ways of women. All that week prior to the Sunday in the long ago I was thinking of having a young woman between these hands. So as to get away I told my father a lie: I told him that a man I met in town was enquiring about a set of harness, and that I might see him again. See how I had her blamed for tellin' me a lie and I was a liar myself. But I lashed the pony all the road home. "You're a blackguard," an old fellow shouted after me.'

The saddler had raised his voice almost to a shout.

The finch. The tick-tock of the clock. The mauve piece of silk. The smell of perfume.

'I'll tell you of my second encounter with a woman,' Shaun said at last, his work ceased, his eyes on the roadway outside, his body accurately balanced on the long-legged stool.

' 'Twas maybe ten years after that. I was twenty-nine or so. I was a full man then. We had a lovely pony mare and I wanted to get her in foal. I saw an advertisement in the county paper by a Welshman or a Scotsman—the family had left England dodging conscription in the First World War—he had a pony sire standing at a stud away in the hills beyond Killarney. I heard great accounts of this sire—an Apaloosa the same as you'd paint him, striped hooves and like a sprinkle of paint-spots on his back. I got John Joe here outside to write a letter in my name.'

The old man looked dully down at the harness beneath him.

'I got an answer back to drive the mare the following Sunday to Brennan's Glen—that's north of Killarney. I was to be there at such and such a time—say half-past three or four in the afternoon. Half-way into the glen there's a narrow byroad leading down to a stream. The road is almost closed in with hazel bushes. Down below it opens out on the bank of the stream. We could do our business there, with no one to make ins or outs on us.

'The following Sunday I was up at cockcrow. I went to Convent Mass. I tackled the mare under the trap, took a bite of food with me and a bottle of new milk, then off I set for the road. I was dressed in my pepper and salt suit. The wheels spinning, the bells ringing, the harness mountin's catching the sun, the mare stepping out as if she knew where she was going—the country people goin' to Mass turned their heads to watch us go by. I bypassed Tralee and came out on the low road. I reached the glen before the time. I turned right and went down by the little road between the hazel trees. At the foot of the boreen there was a strand of gravel on the edge of a pool. I gave the mare a drink. I waited.

'After a while I heard the sound of hooves on the road above. I knew it was a saddle horse by the gait of go. And I knew it was a stallion too. The sound was faint at first. I heard the hooves stop as the horse came to the mouth of the boreen. My mare pricked up her ears. Then, dancing down through the hazel trees, came a girl riding the Apaloosa stallion.

'She could be no more than sixteen or so. She wore jodhpurs, an open shirt and a hunting cap. She took me in at a glance: she looked at the mare, the harness and the trap. The stallion under her began to rear up on the patch of grass at the end of the road. He was whinnying with excitement. The girl controlled him. "Untackle your mare," she shouted as she jumped down off the saddle.

'I had my pony stripped in a jiffy—the harness thrown any old way on the furze bushes. I threw off my jacket too. The girl had her saddle off and was holding her horse by the bridle. The Apaloosa was a beauty.

'Yet, for all my talk, I was innocent. "Where's your groom?" I shouted. She was fighting hard to control the entire horse. "I'm the groom," she shouted. Then, "Look alive, man! Hold your mare."

'I led the mare forward. Whatever way the stallion swung he turned myself and my mare back against the edge of the water. The girl shouted at me for being awkward. She hung on to the stallion as he crested on the mare's hindquarters. He failed the first couple of tries and I almost lost my footing on the gravel. Again the girl shouted at me. I shouted back at her. We were both angry now. I came to my feet as the Apaloosa crested for the third time. There was a terrible hullabaloo, the stallion neighing like mad, his hooves tearing up the gravel, his eyes and nostrils wide, his mouth a mass of froth. I held on to my mare's head till the sire was almost in the mating seat. When he was balanced above, the girl let go the bridle and dived between stallion and mare to ensure that the seed was sown in its proper ground. No groom ever did his job as well as she did. There was a rattle of stones as I was backed by the weight of both animals to the edge of the water. I braced myself against the full weight of the thrust as the stallion fully entered the mare: another backward step onto a slippery stone and I was on the flat of my back in the water with both animals threshing above me. The girl's laughter sounded through the great noise.

'The Apaloosa stallion was first up out of the pool: he was drenched, spent, sweating and shivering. He complained with a low whining.

'I waded in out of the pool. Somehow I didn't care. My mare was horsed. In my imagination I could already see the foal.

'Side by side the young woman and myself washed our hands in the stream. The horses were calm now. She smiled at my soaking clothes. I took off my shoes and squeezed out the stockings. I wrung my shirt too and hung it on the bushes.

'The day was warm. We sat side by side under the hazels. I gave her a sandwich. We had every second drink out of the bottle of milk. She was a dainty eater. After a while my trousers dried out a bit. I was friendly with her now because together we had helped in the making of life. We sat there in the sun. Then I felt that she—how'll I say it?—wanted to play mare to my stallion.

'I knew it by the way she moved, by the way she looked at me, just like those foreign girls looked at you a while ago. I trembled. I was tempted almost beyond the powers of man to resist. You'll laugh at me, but the memory of my waiting at the Wood Cross was uppermost in my mind. That and the way I was brought up: devout, strict, narrow and terrified of life. My mother meant well but before she died, God rest her, she had branded me. My maimed father continued on the same road after she had gone. The missioners too with their crucifixes and candles—I was once refused Absolution for thinkin' too long about a girl. So I was a maimed animal. I didn't then, nor do I now, believe in looseness between man and woman but I felt that there should be a middle road. Nature had bound me to one law: rearing, training and faith had bound me to another.

'When I made no move, I saw that she had turned against me. We stood up. As I counted the fee into her hand her eyes were full of contempt. Money for services rendered! She didn't bother to count the coins, just dug the fistful deep into the pocket of her riding britches. She turned on her heels and walked away from me. When I showed that I wanted to help her with the saddle girth she muttered something which meant that she could do without me. Up with her then into the saddle. She drew hard on the reins, the stallion whirled on the stones and went rockin' and grindin' away out of sight. I heard them reach the road above. The sound of hooves died away into the distance. The young woman was out of my life. But not out of my mind!'

*   *   *

The student studied the boards of the old counter. His mind shuttled between the old man's confession and the incident of the two women who had left the shop. What was it stopped me speaking French when they were present? he asked himself. Fear of ridicule? Fear of being involved? Fear of crossing a boundary? And again, where was it I have heard or read something like the old's second story? If I let my mind sag into nothingness perhaps a solution will emerge from the subconscious.

Tick-tock. Squeak. The student glanced at the mauve handkerchief, then secretly inhaled. He came to his feet and replaced the shapeless lump of wax on the counter. With a quiet word to the old man he left the shop. He walked thoughtfully up the deserted street.

He found that he was now able to see his options a little more clearly. He groped towards the realization that it wasn't a stark choice between the making of horses or humans on one hand and the womanless calm of the sanctuary and presbytery on the other. Nor was it the polarity of perfume and incense nor that of sacrifice and stallion foam. There were intermediate shades, scents and sounds that could be interpreted as experience. He felt better already. He now had something solid by way of precedent to cope with.

In the canyon of the street bright sunlight held half the roadway. The other half was in comparative darkness. The student chose to walk on the pavement that was shadow-black. He pictured himself as Morocco before the caskets. Yet that was not the reference he sought.

Of a sudden he had it!

The fertile plain of La Beauce stretching to the gates of Chartres. Françoise Fouan, fourteen, her face the colour of a hazel nut leading her red and white cow La Coliche.
La Coliche is on heat. She is being taken to the bull at La Borderie.

The girl waits in vain at the farm.
Jean Macquart, twenty-nine, ex-carpenter, ex-soldier doffs his seed
bag, leaves the ploughed field and comes to assist her.
César, the Black Friesian bull, enters the cobbled yard.
La Coliche lows a welcome.
César mounts La Coliche. The cow is big. The bull is small.
When he cannot manage, the girl adroitly takes command.

The student is pleased at his power of recall. It's from *La Terre* by Emile Zola, he says almost aloud. The young man's eyes indicate thoughtfulness as he recalls that there is a priest in the story too, Abbé Godard, fat, red-necked and inclined to puff if he walks any distance.

The student turns into the street of cutstone cottages where he lives with his widowed mother. Tomorrow, he tells himself, I will come to a decision.

The Gap of Life

As the clock beneath the steeple in the square rustily banged four an old man emerged from a cottage set on a hillock on the edge of the town. It was a midsummer morning with the pale blue sky pricked with waning stars.

Wearing a long black overcoat over his pyjamas, the old fellow shuffled forward on misshapen carpet slippers. He glanced along the cobbled ramp that rose from beside his doorway and vanished in a pathway that ran between the cottage gable and the high wall of a demesne. He moved to the kerbside and, stepping down on to the narrow roadway, glanced cautiously up and down.

The final humming of the clock strokes below had thinned out into silence.

Standing in the road and shading his eyes with his bladed hand so as to shut out the light of a nearby street lamp, the old man looked downhill for an appreciable space of time. At last he lowered his hand, shook his head and made as if to return to the doorway of the cottage.

The lock-lock of a bicycle straining as it moved uphill towards him caused him to hurry indoors.

The cyclist, a young man of twenty or so, was whistling softly. Just before he reached the cottage he dismounted and walked along the roadway, wheeling his bicycle as he came. Noticing that the door of the cottage was not fully closed, he slowed his pace somewhat and kept his eyes on the door. Gradually his footsteps idled to a halt. Resting his elbow on the saddle of the bicycle, he continued to watch the door.

'Hey!' he called out at last. 'You in there—are you all right?'

There was no reply.

The young man backed his bicycle until he was abreast of the doorway.

'You in there,' he said, raising his voice, 'are you all right?'

22

There was a long pause. At last, speaking from the darkness just inside the door, the old man said in an even tone, 'Yes, I'm all right.'

The young man remained as he was for a few moments. 'Is there anything the matter with you?' he asked, and then added rather lamely, 'If it's the time you want it's just four o'clock in the morning.'

There was no reply.

The young man muttered to himself and made as if to wheel his bicycle onwards. Then he stopped, propped the bicycle against the old stone kerb, and stepping on to the raised pathway in front of the cottage walked cautiously back until he was again almost abreast of the doorway. He peered in.

'You still there?' he asked.

'Yes, I'm here.'

'Are you sick? Or are you one of those fellows who can't sleep?'

'I'm not ill,' the voice said. 'And as a rule I'm a sound sleeper.'

The young man hesitated, then said gruffly, 'If that's the way you want it that's the way you'll get it.' He moved towards his bicycle but again turned on seeing the old man emerge and shuffle down on to the roadway.

Again the old fellow shaded his eyes with his hand as he looked downhill.

The young man examined the other—his squashed slippers, his frayed pyjama ends, his old-fashioned black velours-trimmed overcoat, his hollowed neck and grey hair. 'Expecting someone?' he asked suddenly.

'I don't think anyone will come. I don't think they'll even send a message.'

'Who won't come? Eh? Who won't send a message?'

'*She* won't come . . . And those in charge—*they* won't send a message.'

'Those in charge of what?'

'Those in charge of her.'

'Her?'

'Yes, her.'

'I see,' the young man said in a puzzled tone of voice.

The old fellow turned and said solemnly, 'Then again, she may even be going.'

'Going where?'

'Ah!' the old fellow said with a sad satisfaction. 'That's the most difficult question in the world to answer.'

With a smile, 'Ever hear what the chap said about the bus or the woman?' the young man said.

'No.'

' "If you miss a bus or a woman," this chap said, "don't worry your head for there's always another one coming!" ' The young man shouted with laughter at his own joke.

'I won't have that talk,' the old man said sternly. 'Be on your way whoever you are!'

'Whoever I am, is it? Easy now, old fellow! Simon is my name. Simple Simon was my nickname at school but whoever'd buy me as a fool would want his money back. I'm a fitter sent here to do a repair job on your creamery. Now, tell me your trouble.'

'I've no trouble.'

'Then why are you out of your bed at this hour of a summer morning?' In a kindly tone, 'Out with it!'

The old man paused, his face crafty. 'I'd tell you only . . .'

'Only what?'

'There are generations between us.'

'What if there are? I'm human too. Look, I've two hands, two legs and one head just like yourself. Other organs as well.'

'I didn't seek your company,' the old man said.

Simon turned wearily away. Then turning around, 'It's your daughter, isn't it?'

'I've no children alive.'

'It's your sister?'

'Not her either.'

'The old woman who keeps house for you?' As the old man shook his head, 'Who is it then?'

'It's my wife . . . she's ill.'

'Where is she?'

'In St Joseph's Hospital.' He vaguely indicated the point in the landscape below where the hospital lay.

'Is she *very* ill?'

'She won't last this night,' the old man said quietly. Then, 'Come here, son. See that faint light in the hospital window? That's where she is. And I'm here . . . and not beside her at all. Now she and I who have been together so long are going our separate ways, and I can't help thinking . . .'

'What is it you can't help thinking?'

'. . . that her hand should be in mine as she goes through the gap of life. I spoke to the Reverend Matron of the hospital . . .'

'What did *she* say?'

'She said, "Off home with you now, Timothy, and we'll do all that's needed." I asked the doctor: he said the same. They didn't mean to give offence, but they didn't understand.'

There was a short silence in which the old man lifted his face to the sky and added, 'My wife was a great scholar.'

'A scholar?'

'A great woman to read stories.'

'What kind of stories?'

'Best of all she liked legends. Legends from the east and from the west. She never grew tired of reading the story of Orpheus aloud for me.'

'I never heard that story.'

'It's a story from ancient Greece. Orpheus called up his woman from the underworld. Her hand in his, they walked upwards towards the light. And then, because he looked into her eyes too soon, he lost her in the gap of life.'

'Yes?'

' "Eurydice!" he shouted just like that. But she was gone.' The old man's voice trembled as he added, 'I'm a kind of Orpheus now calling on Betty through the morning hours. "Betty," I say, "Timothy is here! Give me your hand as you go out the gap of life . . .'

'Sssh!' Simon said for the old fellow had been shouting. He added, 'Will I stay here for a while and keep you company?'

'I'll be all right.'

'Is there anything I can do for you?'

'There's nothing *you* can do for me.'

'Why not?'

'I don't wish to be rude, but *you* don't seem to be the kind of young man to do what I want done.'

'What is it you want done?'

'You'd only poke fun at me. It's different manners today. To you and those of your day women are playthings to be used and thrown aside.'

'Tell me what you want or I'll be angry with you.'

There was a long pause. Timothy examined the face of the

young man. 'You promise not to laugh at me?' he asked at last.

'I promise.'

'The hospital gate is locked. But if a lively fellow was to go around by this cobbled laneway between my cottage and the demesne wall and then travel along the railway line he'd find a chestnut tree with branches that dip over the hospital wall. That way he could get in.'

'Go on.'

'He could steal through the kitchen garden, pass the long rick of turf, come around by the gable of the building and then he'd maybe find the third window from the end . . .'

'That's where she is, is it?'

'Aye. The young man could even stand outside and peep in. And if he saw what I think he'd see, without himself being seen . . .'

'Yes?'

'He could open his hand like this, as if he was taking a woman's hand in his. And then he could say "Eurydice!" '

'The woman inside—how can she hear him?'

'It doesn't matter whether she hears or not,' Timothy said with intensity. As Simon shook his head, the old fellow added, 'Don't you see? 'Twill be almost the same as if I was there myself.'

'I think you should take the advice of the doctor and the nun,' Simon said wearily.

'Good morning to you, son,' the old man said. He turned his face towards the cottage door.

Simon took his bicycle and made as if to move away. He paused. 'Eurydice,' he said half to himself, 'that's a fancy name.' Addressing the old man, 'Tell me—how could there be such closeness between you and her?'

'From being together always, we grew to have the one mind.'

'The one mind?'

'If we were quiet in each other's company I'd say, "You're thinking of the day we went together in the wagonette to Fenit Pier?" '

'Would you be right?'

'Yes! Another time if we were walking in silence along a country road, I'd say, "It's your Uncle Jim in Adelaide?" '

'Would you be right again?'

'I'd be always right. And then in the morning hours if she

26

trembled and shouted "Orpheus!" through her sleep I'd know she was afraid of this very morning. Then I'd take her hand in mine and she'd be comforted. Women can see beyond the grave far clearer than us men . . .'

The old man fell silent for a while. Then in a humble tone he said, 'I'm sorry for troubling you. You'll likely have a hard day's work in front of you. Goodbye, son.'

He moved towards the door of the cottage.

'Wait!' Simon called out, placing his bicycle against the kerb. 'What is it?'

'The third window from the gable end? Eurydice?' As Timothy nodded, Simon said, 'I'll be back before you know it!'

Briskly he removed the clips from his trouser-ends, buttoned up his jacket and ran up the cobbled ramp.

The old man listened as the light sound of the sprinting footsteps grew fainter and fainter. He remained as he was for a few moments. He then shuffled to the point where the base of the cobbled ramp merged into the ground. Here the top of the little stone wall that edged the ramp was shaped like a low black polished stool with a railing of ribbon iron behind it. Facing the roadway, the old fellow seated himself on the dark stone and shrivelled up his body until it seemed lost in the folds of his overcoat. He leaned his poll against the railing. His eyes closed.

The wheel of the heavens swung through all the intermediate stages of tint and hue between pale blue and young apple-green. Stars and street lights waned and the natural light of day began to come into its own. Sunk on his breast the old man's head gently fell and rose in sleep.

★   ★   ★

A motor-car stopped some distance away. There was the sound of muted mingled laughter—the deep laughter of a man and the rippling laughter of a young woman. There were low-keyed goodbyes as the car drove off. The sound of the young woman's footsteps hurriedly approaching failed to awaken the old fellow.

The girl wore a dark cape above a flowing evening dress of pink chiffon. She moved with fluency. Seeing the sleeping figure she stopped in front of it, then, placing her hand on the old man's shoulder, shook him gently. 'Sir!' she breathed. As Timothy's eyes opened, the girl said, 'You'll catch your death sitting there!'

'Did he come back?' The old man's widening eyes showed fear.

'Did who come back?'

'The young man who owns the bicycle.'

'There's no one here.'

'He went on a message for me.'

'What message?'

'He should be back long ago. What time is it?'

Just then the town clock struck five. Together the old man and the girl counted the strokes.

'Five!' Timothy said in dismay.

'He must return for his bicycle,' the girl said. 'Was it an important message?'

'Yes.'

'Perhaps I can deliver it instead of him?'

'No! You can't deliver it at all.' There was a pause in which Timothy first looked dully about him and then up into the girl's face. 'I should know you,' he said. 'What's your name?'

'You know me, Timothy. I'm Hanna.'

'Hanna what?'

'Hanna Meehan. I'm a daughter of Tom Meehan, the land steward. I live in the side-lodge of the demesne. I'm home on holidays from the University.'

'I remember you now,' Timothy said without conviction.

'You used to give me apples from your tree when I was small. "Sweeteens" you called them. Remember?'

The old man's face opened in joyous clarity. 'Oh!' he said. 'Hanna Meehan—I have you now. You were so . . .' His hand crept out to indicate a child. 'Dear God, are you grown so big?'

The girl laughed merrily. 'I'm grown so big,' she said, then added, 'What's bothering you?'

'The madness of the old, that's all. Were you dancing, girl?'

'Yes.'

'Did you enjoy yourself?'

The girl's mouth made an indeterminate moue. 'It was my first dress-dance,' she said with something of disappointment to her tone. She caught the old man's hands in hers. 'Your hands are cold. What are you waiting for?'

'My wife is ill in St Joseph's. I couldn't sleep with thinking of

28

her, so I sent a young man who was passing to see if she was gone or not . . .'

'I can phone from the lodge and ask the night nurse how she is. When I come back with news it will ease your mind.'

The old man shook his head. 'My message is different,' he said.

The girl's sharp ears caught the sound of someone running in the laneway. 'He's coming,' she said.

Simon came quickly round the gable-end of the cottage and on to the cobbled ramp. He stopped short on seeing the girl with the old man. Still keeping his eyes on her, he came forward; he seemed somehow to resent finding his former intimacy with the old fellow broken.

'Well, son?' Timothy began.

'I found the tree,' Simon said with obvious reluctance. 'I crossed the wall. I came through the kitchen garden. I passed the rick of turf and turned the gable of the building. I stopped in the shadow outside the third window from the end.'

'Yes?'

'The light in the ward was burning low. Her bed was just inside the window.'

'Yes?'

'I stood there for a while. A nun dressed in white came along inside. She wore a crucifix and her rosary was rattling. She drew back the screen around the bed. A nurse came then and took the woman's pulse. She tightened her lips and nodded. The nun took a prayer book out of her skirt and began to read softly. The nurse answered the prayer.'

'What was it she read?'

'The Litany . . .'

'I see. Go on.'

'It went on and on. I thought 'twould never end. Then it was the *De Profundis*—"Out of the depths I have cried to thee, O Lord!" When that was finished another patient called. The two women put back the screen and went away. I watched your wife. She was breathing hard. 'Twas plain to see that she was stumbling through the gap of life.'

'What then?' the old man asked softly.

Simon walked a little distance apart. The old fellow glanced at Hanna and then said in a firm tone, 'Answer me! A woman always understands.'

Simon, his face averted, kept looking into the distance. At last he spoke. 'I raised the window slowly. I stretched in my hand and caught her by the hand. Her hand was sweating and yet 'twas icy cold. Then in a loud whisper, "Eurydice!" I said.'

'Go on!'

'Her breathing stopped. "Eurydice!" I said again. Then her hand tightened upon mine.'

'Tell out God's naked truth!' The old man's voice had exploded into a cracked shout. 'That you may be crucified if you tell a lie!'

'God's naked sacred truth!' The young man had spun round and his voice came riding over the old man's outburst. 'I tell you that her hand tightened on mine.' There was a pause. Then he added quietly, 'She gathered herself together then. She quivered a little . . .'

'Yes?'

'Then slowly she let go the breath. I waited for another breath. It never came. Her hand fell loosely by the bedside. I drew back my hand. I lowered the window without sound and again I stood in the shadow.'

'What else?' said Timothy.

'The nun came back. She took the pulse. She looked at the nurse and shook her head. Then she drew the sheet up over the woman's face.'

Timothy moved slowly to one side and looked downhill. 'You played your part,' he said slowly. He looked up at the morning sky. As if speaking to himself, he said, 'I suppose I should say "Lord have mercy on her." But there are others who have said that.' He turned to face the young man and the young woman. 'Ye can be going now. Thanks to the pair of ye.'

'Can I make tea for you?' Hanna asked.

'Not if you don't want it yourself.'

'I don't need it, thank you.'

The old man nodded his head as if in thanks. Unexpectedly he raised his voice and began to sing quaveringly:

> 'Thou hast gone from me, Eurydice,
> Now my life is dark with fear . . .'

As his voice broke off, Hanna moved to mid-road and looked up at the eastern sky. 'One last star left,' she said; then, 'I have never been out at this hour of the morning before. So

30

many wonderful things must happen while we're asleep.'

'She had the loveliest and the queerest sayings,' the old man said.

'What kind of sayings?' Simon broke in.

'Sayings that had to do with men and women, with life and death, with hatred and love. Things I could hardly tell a soul.'

'You say a woman always understands,' Hanna said softly.

'That's true,' Timothy conceded. After thinking for a while he added, 'She used to say that a man wants but a woman wants to be wanted. And she used to say too . . .'

'Yes?' from Simon.

'About the things that call love into being—there's a big word for them—she used to say that the greatest stimulator of all was death.'

'Why should she say a thing like that?' Simon asked.

'I couldn't be sure. I think it had something to do with it being the nature of woman to replace that which is lost. Will I tell ye where I first met her?'

'Yes,' both said softly together.

'I first met her in a wakeroom. An old man was dead. Betty was going around the room carrying a silver tray of wine. I'll never forget her young face above that silver tray of wine.' The old man turned and said vehemently, 'I could have stretched out my hand and placed it on the corpse's face . . . and yet there was Betty, her face above the silver tray of wine and her two eyes whispering, "Replace! Replace that which has been lost!" '

'What else would she say?' Hanna asked.

The old man gave a short whinny of laughter. 'She said a woman was most truly a woman when, alone, she stopped to watch her reflection in a mirror. And at that she'd laugh at me and tell me to watch people.'

'What do you mean—watch people?' Simon asked.

' "If you watch every move they make you'll maybe understand"—those were her words,' the old man said.

'Understand what?' Simon asked.

'All about people, of course. What way their minds work. She'd tell me especially to watch how they moved. "A man," she'd say, "as he walks, with every step he strikes the world a blow. But a woman, as she walks, she strokes the air just like you'd stroke a cat. These small things," she'd tell me, "are everything." '

'Everything?' softly from Hanna.

Timothy went on as if speaking from reverie. 'She was a full woman to me,' he said, in proud and measured tones. 'And in her own lovely cautious way she taught me how to be a full man to her. And so for me now it seems that there are treasures everywhere, treasures in the time that's gone and in the time that's as yet unrolled. Because of her I'm richer than Croesus in my memories.'

'What do you mean—these things are everything?' Simon insisted.

'And so they are,' the old fellow said. 'Aren't they among God's most precious gifts to man?' He looked directly at Simon. 'Son,' he said, 'the clock of time is ticking on. Now maybe it's your turn to sit in the wakeroom of the world and see a woman's face above a silver tray of wine.' Turning to the girl, 'And you, Hanna Meehan, pay heed to me! A man driving in a motor-car, every girl he meets on the road looks through the windscreen straight and true. And her eyes always find his. And with her eyes the girl asks one question and one question only.'

'What question?' Simon asked impatiently.

'Don't tell him!' the girl broke in.

'What question does the girl ask?' Simon insisted.

'Her question is a straight and natural one—"Is this the man who since the beginning of time was meant to fertilize my body?" All the words in the world lead to that question.'

Simon roared with laughter. As the girl turned and looked at him with hatred in her eyes the young man broke off shamefacedly.

Timothy shuffled closer to Simon.

'Son,' he said, not without sadness, 'you haven't even learned the ABC of life.' Turning away and speaking as it were to himself he went on, 'Lord have mercy on the dead, is it? No, by God, but Lord have mercy on the living . . . on those with souls of smoke and bodies made of cork and minds like Punch and Judy shows.' Sensing that Simon was still smiling, the old man rounded upon him. 'Don't dare smile at me, my son!' he said in a loud voice. 'I tell you that very many live out their lives frightened by cardboard giants towering above them in the dark. Heed me, the pair of you,' he spoke now in a tone of pleading, 'heed me, although I'm a cracked old man snared by a legend from the Grecian day and by the green morning walking up the sky . . .'

He looked about him in a puzzled manner as if there was

32

something else he had forgotten to say. Then he shuffled forward and entered the cottage, quietly closing the door behind him.

Hanna moved a few steps and leaned her back against the low wall beside the stone stool on which the old man had fallen asleep. She pushed her head well back so that her hair rested against the narrow iron rail. Her long white throat was seen. Simon moved a few faltering steps: he hardly knew whether to go or stay.

'Him!' he said at last. The girl made no reply.

'Him! Would he be a wise man or a fool?' he tried again.

'He's wise,' Hanna said.

Simon pondered this for a few moments. 'He made a queer class of mood just now,' he said then.

'Did he?'

'Aye, he did. But . . . I feel it going away from me now like a tide moving back into the sea.' He laughed oddly. 'And I'm not certain that I want that mood to go.' He looked at the girl, then ventured to say, 'Did you meet anyone special at the dance?'

After a pause, 'No!'

'Oh!' Simon watched the girl for a few seconds and said, 'This mood that I was talking about—can it be captured and brought back again?'

'Moods come and go,' the young woman said.

' "Souls of smoke, bodies of cork, and minds . . ." minds like what?'

'Like Punch and Judy shows.'

'Punch was the man, eh?'

'Punch was the man.'

'He said that all words lead to it—what did he mean by that?'

'I don't know—unless you could guess, yourself.'

After a pause, 'Salmon!' the young man blurted in a loud voice. 'There's a word that just came into my head. Salmon! How does the word salmon lead to what he was talking about?'

Hanna did not reply.

'You hear me, woman?'

'I hear you. That word might remind you of . . .'

'Of what?'

'Of a hen salmon fighting her way upstream against a torrent . . .'

'Aye! Fighting her way upstream to meet her destiny,' the young man said. Then, with an added sense of discovery, 'Or beating her head against the gravel of the redd as she prepares to spawn.'

There was a short silence. Then with a suppressed cry of triumph Simon said, 'By God, I'm close to something that has dodged me all these years.' He turned and looked at the girl. Shyly he asked, 'If I sat there beside you would you tell me the story?'

'What story?'

'You know well what story!'

'I do.'

'Then why did you pretend not to know?'

'Protocol.'

'What the hell is protocol?'

'The right way and the wrong.' Her eyes fell. Not without wryness she added, 'Protocol says that the man must ask, and that the woman must answer as if she didn't quite understand . . .'

'And then?'

'And then she must lead him on and on until at last she's completely sure.'

'Hey!' Simon shouted as if in discovery. 'I'll ask you so! Tell me the story of Orpheus and Eurydice.' He moved swiftly towards the ramp and squatted at her feet. He looked up into her face.

The girl began with a demure certainty. 'Orpheus, son of a god, had the gift of music and of song. Wild beasts would turn and listen as he played upon his lute. The birds of the forest would fall silent at the first note he played at the break of day. He took Eurydice as his wife. She died and went down to Hades in the dark. He pleaded for her life and at last was told, "You may go down into the underworld and find your wife. But do not look upon her face until you reach the mortal world above." And so . . .'

'And so?'

'He took with him a ball of yarn and unrolled it as he went down among the caves. At last in the darkness he reached her shade. "Eurydice!" he cried and handed her the thread. "Orpheus!" she said. Following the thread, the man and the woman walked towards the light, step after step upwards towards the light . . .'

The girl stood erect. Her face was averted. The young man rose and waited for her to resume.

'Just as they had reached the gap of life . . .' The girl's voice broke off suddenly.

Gently and slowly Simon took her by the shoulder points and turned her round so that the first light of the morning sun touched her features. 'You're crying, woman,' he said softly.

Angrily the girl tore herself free. As she raced up the ramp and hurried along the pathway between the demesne wall and the cottage gable her voice reached him in tatters of anger and disappointment. 'The fool!' she cried. 'He broke the gods' taboo!'

Simon stood for an uncomprehending moment or two. Then he heard the voice of the old man singing faintly from the cottage.

> 'Thou has gone from me, Eurydice,
> Now my life is dark with fear,
> Grief and woe fill my soul
> Nevermore thy voice to hear
> Nevermore thy voice to hear . . .'

Simon turned from the closed door and glanced at the cobbled pathway along which the girl had fled. After a time he moved to mid-road and looked down towards the hospital building now illumined by the rays of the risen sun. Wearily he moved to the steps at the base of the ramp, set each of his shoes in turn on the end of the low wall and replaced his bicycle clips.

He then wheeled his bicycle onto the road. Putting his footsole on the near pedal, he hopped briskly on to the saddle. Softly he resumed his whistling as he rode away.

The Miler

'Ave Maria: Guests Welcome,' the sign said. Reading its white letters on a black wooden shield, I smiled: the 'Ave Maria' could well have been an invocation of the Virgin, imploring her to guard the house against incontinent guests.

Leaving the car, I peered down over the fuchsia hedge at the large building that lay below road level and which was now outlined against the evening sea.

Obviously a converted barracks or coastguard station; a few faded sycamore trees grew in the lee of its walls, their autumn leaves robbing the stonework of a little of its austerity. On the hillside to my right a ploughman and a pair of horses had halted at the bottom of a newly-broken field: city-bred, I thought late August an odd time of year for a ploughman to be at work.

I am a runner and, at that time, I was training for the Irish mile. Whenever circumstances allowed, I combined my annual holidays with a stint of dedicated training. Thus, that late summer and early autumn, I had driven southward along the west coast of Ireland. Whenever I came upon a stretch of roadway above the sea, I left the car and, peeling off my track-suit which I wore over my vest and trunks, jogged for a mile or so away from the car and in the direction from which I had come. Then, turning about, I jogged back to the car and, having run a further mile in the direction in which the car was facing, finished with a sharp sprint as I returned to the vehicle.

This routine I repeated twice, or even three times, during the day. I thought this method of reaching fitness much more interesting than slogging at twilight through the suburbs of Dublin.

I was now in the extreme south-west of Munster—in an area where a dour rampart of cliff was broken only by untenanted coves. The traditional prevalence of smuggling, together with the folk-memory of a French invasion fleet in the area, must have necessitated, in British days, the building of such a stronghold. In later times, the building, then fallen into disuse, had likely been put up for auction. Still looking at the sign, I reckoned it a brave man—or woman—who had undertaken the conversion of such a fortress to a guesthouse.

Stay there for a night? I pondered the question. 'Ave Maria! Guests welcome,' I repeated to myself as if it were a prayer.

Then came a surprise, for on walking a few yards along the roadway I saw eight or nine motor-cars parked under the sycamore trees below. The tourist plates on the vehicles, white, red, striped and blue, told me that, for the most part, the cars were from the Continent.

With a start, I realized that it was the Saturday preceding a bank holiday and that if I did not make up my mind at once I might be forced to spend the night huddled up in the back seat of the vehicle.

I coasted down a driveway between a rout of rhododendrons and grated to a halt under the grey-green stone walls. Above me were slits of latticed windows with corner turrets set at all sorts of angles, whence, very likely, a view could be had of the sea and the coastline to the north and south.

I left the car and entered the outer whitewashed hall of the guesthouse. Knocking on the black-painted knocker on the inner glass door I waited. The house seemed lifeless.

As I banged on the knocker a second time, a sweaty-faced girl, a wing of her black hair sliding across her eyes, opened the door. The smell of good cooking rode out over the smell of stone. The girl looked wide-eyed at me.

'Could I have an evening meal, bed and breakfast?' I asked.

Before the words were fully out of my mouth, 'We're full,' the girl blurted. 'Could I see the manager?' I asked, to be answered all of a rush, 'There's no one, only the missus!' 'The missus?' I repeated and again the girl came full pelt with 'We're full! We're turnin' 'em away all evenin'!'

She drew back a little and waited for me to be off.

But I was resolved to try to impose my will on the young woman, as so often I had tried to impose my will on my rivals in a race! The smell of cooking had sharpened my appetite: the girl, however, now seemed determined to shut the door in my face.

I pretended to yield a point. 'Ask your missus if she would give me a meal,' I said. 'Then, if there is still no room, I'll push on.'

'I tell you we're full,' the girl repeated. At which I said sternly, 'Please ask your missus!' The girl, a wiggle of fear in her eyes, closed the door and thumped away. I was left alone in the flag-stoned hall.

With the sound of the sea for company, I waited. After a time I turned and tapped softly with my fingertips on the face of a large barometer hanging on the wall. The glass was falling. I had already found a touch of coldness about my shoulder-blades and had heard the faint sob of rain in the evening breeze. A foghorn boomed in the faraway: recalling my map I wondered which of the three great rocks the sound came from—the Bull, the Cow, or the Calf.

The girl re-opened the door; her dilated eyes indicated that I should follow her. An oil lamp, not yet alight, hung from the ceiling of the inner hall.

Entering the dining-room, its walls of stone with whitewashed edgings on the doors and windows and a candle casting its wan light on each table, the girl glanced at the guests already seated. It was as if she were apologizing for the presence of an intruder dressed in a track-suit. As she made to lead me to a side-table which stood in the semi-darkness of an alcove, my spread palms indicated that I wished to wash my hands: this necessitated my following the girl along a corridor and entering an old-fashioned lamplit bathroom in which stood a large bath-tub with the feet of a monster. However, the water racing into the large hand-basin was almost boiling and the towels were clean.

I returned to the dining-room; from the alcove in which I sat I could observe the greater part of the dim room. In all there were about sixteen or seventeen guests present. I listened to a murmur in different languages: German I recognized, Swedish too, and after a time the bird-like peckings of French. As far as I could tell I was the only Irish person present.

The day's exercise had given me a sharp appetite. The meal was a good one. First, onion soup with pot-oven bread and homemade butter, followed by boiled salmon with parsley sauce. For main course I had roast lamb with mint sauce and potatoes that were balls of flour—the whole followed by a pleasant dessert of carrageen sea-moss and cream. Finally, I had cheddar cheese, cream crackers and strong black coffee.

My blue track-suit rendering me inconspicuous, I continued to listen to the quiet chatter of the other guests around whom darkness was now gathering.

Now and again there was a dull flash of silver in the half-light of the room and the faint gurgle of wine being poured. The maid who had opened the door for me served the tables. Once I glimpsed her taking a laden tray of food from hands outstretched from a nearby corridor.

By the time the meal had ended it was dark outside. The maid returned to the dining-room, and lighted successively four oil-lamps clamped to the walls.

I drew out the end of the meal to the full, gambling on the fact that the later the evening the greater was the likelihood of my being allowed to stay. The maid kept casting me an anxious eye, as if telling me to pay my bill and be off. When, in decency, I could delay no longer I stood up and walked towards the door of the dining-room; the other guests barely raised their heads to see me go. In the inner hallway, where by now the overhead oil lamp was lit, the girl, chit in hand, was waiting. Groping slowly in my pocket-book I asked suddenly: 'Could I see the proprietress?'

'We're full!'

'Could I see her just the same?'

The girl mumbled something, then moved through an opening shaped like a Gothic archway. I heard the put-put of heavy raindrops falling on the gravel outside.

'Yes?'

I turned. A youngish woman, a little flushed, obviously as a result of cooking the meal, was standing before me. The lamp hung directly above my head, so that for a moment or two I could not help noting the restrained vividness of her face. I had a sense of remotely seeing her well-tapered legs. 'Thank you for a pleasant meal,' I began; then, 'Could you put me up for the night? I'm not particular where I sleep.'

Adroitly the woman had moved around me until the light was falling fully on my face and body. She glanced with interest at my track-suit. 'Every room is full,' she said a little hesitantly and in a musical voice, 'but if you drive on twenty miles or so . . .'

'I've slept rough before,' I told her, now holding the twenty-pound note in my hand. Risking a laugh, I added, 'I'm strong and healthy.'

The woman looked from the note to my face, then paused to listen to the roar of a thunder shower on the gravel outside. Again she looked at me. Rather hesitantly, she began, 'If you don't mind sharing a room . . .'

'Not at all!'

There was a pause, in which the woman again looked at me carefully.

'It's difficult to explain,' she said quietly. 'Your room-mate is old. He's a priest. Rather nervy, too. He won't bother you. He'll come in late and will be gone before you wake up in the morning. Whatever happens, you mustn't disturb him.'

'I'll be careful,' I said.

'Very well.'

The woman turned; taking a lit candle from a table in a nearby passageway, she led the way up a flight of pine stairs, along a corridor, then up a second flight of stairs. At last we reached a small strongly made door, which, when opened, showed a step down into a bedroom.

Entering at her heels I saw that the place seemed larger than it really was—this possibly because of the fact that the floor of the room was on three levels. One was the level on which we stood, on the left of which was a narrow divan bed; in one corner, diagonally opposite the door and a step up, was a recess in a turret, obviously a place designed for the observation of the sea below. The third level was reached by a step down into an embrasure. This last held a spacious low-slung bed with a dark curtain half-drawn across the front of it. The bed filled almost all the space in the recess.

The room as a whole seemed medievally intimate: the furniture of dark mahogany showed up starkly against the white walls. The place also had a stage unity which was enhanced by the shifting candlelight. In a wall-niche was a statue of the Virgin in coloured wood—Bavarian, I guessed.

Superimposed on the remote smell of unusedness that hung about the place was another smell I could neither isolate nor define; it could well have been incense—that is, if the priest were not retired, or silenced. On the edge of the circle of the candlelight I noticed a square mirror which I recognized as French, and on a slender-legged table beneath it a graceful blue jug and water ewer —the neck and handle of the ewer suggesting a sailing swan. The narrow divan was not made up: this bed was clearly meant for me and the bed in the embrasure was where the priest slept. 'I'll have it made up for you at once,' the woman said with reference to the divan. She indicated an old-fashioned candle-sconce with a box of matches in it. 'Remember where it is: it may be hard to find it in the darkness!'

I murmured my thanks. We went downstairs. After taking my overnight bag and suit from the boot of the car I had a bath—rather belatedly now that the meal was over, I told myself—then putting on my tweed suit I went for a stroll before going to bed.

The shower had ended. The evening air smelled of autumn. There was a fitful moon showing at intervals in an angry sky. I could see the outlines of a pier dark against the silver of sea-water, so I moved downwards along a pathway that led towards it. At the pier-head a hunched-up old man stood looking out on to the water. I stood beside him. Above us was a huge boulder cloven as by an enormous axe; moving a few steps so that the rock no longer obscured my view I saw to the south a dim cluster of lights—obviously a village on yet another peninsula.

After we had exchanged a few words on the weather, the old man absent-mindedly told me the legend of a giant splitting the rock, and added, 'I'm watching the seals!'

I then saw what I took to be a seal swimming in the moon-glitter of the sea. 'May Christ sweep you off the face of the map!' the old man shouted. 'You have all my salmon carried.' At the sound of the raised voice the seal seemed to tread water. For a while its sagacious head was turned in our direction.

'Dangerous bastards!' the old fellow went on. 'They attacked me one day in a cave.' He indicated a cavern in the cliffside. 'Out there on the Skelligs Rock they couple, face to face—like man and woman!' He vaguely gestured to the Rock far out in the sea mist.

We lapsed into companionable silence. Far to the north a lighthouse flared intermittently. After a time three tinker girls appeared, seemingly out of nowhere: two of the three used the third, who appeared to be a simpleton, as a foil. All three indicated wantonness in the manner in which they begged for money and in the violent way in which they pushed one another when they were near us. The foolish one—she could have been eighteen—

as a result of one such push cannoned off me so that I had to catch her before she went sprawling. I shall not readily forget the contrast between her ripe body and the idiocy of her face. As, for a moment, I held her close, she seemed to be struggling up to a new kind of understanding. It was a fleeting, but for me, an illuminating moment. Then the old man beside me raised his stick and all three ran off screaming into the darkness.

As a result of our shared indignation—his real enough, mine simulated—the old man and I were now on closer terms.

'You're staying up above?' he asked, indicating the bulk of the guesthouse. On my admitting that I was, I began to question him. According to him, the woman (he called her a girl) who owned the place was something of a mystery. 'Young enough but reserved. She has a touch of a foreign accent but somehow I'd say she's Irish away back. She turned up here from nowhere a few years ago. She seems to have neither kith nor kin. The next thing workmen were tearin' the Old Fort—for so we call the barracks —asunder, herself dartin' in and out watchin' the work. Then she opens a guesthouse—mostly foreigners stop there. With only an orphanage girl to help her she is makin' a brave effort to make a go of the place.

'The troubles in the North aren't helping her one bit,' the old fellow went on; then, without a trace of malice towards me, he added, 'You'd want to be stone mad, or from Europe itself, to come here at all! And madder still to stop here—even for a night!' As I laughed, 'But give the lassie above her due, she's a trier! She'd work herself to the bone to earn a shilling. Tryin' too hard, maybe. But she doesn't mix nor meddle with anyone hereabouts. Nor we with her!'

'Who is the priest?' I asked suddenly. 'What priest?' the old fellow snapped. 'Isn't there a priest staying there?' I asked lightly. 'The Pope of Rome could be staying there for all I know,' the old man said. We dropped the subject.

*   *   *

When I returned the house seemed asleep. It was as if the ranked cars resented the sound of my footsteps on the gravel. I turned the black knob on the white door and went in. The wall lamp in the inner hall, its wick turned low, showed me my way to the foot of the stairs. The staircase itself was a sounding box: twice I knocked my toecap loudly against one of the risers. Mercifully there were no creaks.

Half-way up, I thought I heard a noise below. I stopped and had a vague sense of a someone stealing out to verify that I had returned. Reaching my room, I groped forward to the table on which the candle-sconce lay, drew a match against the side of the matchbox and set the flame to the wick. The smell of wax, sulphur, dampness, sea air, and the remote odour that could have been incense—or fresh yeast—touched my nostrils. My watch told me that it was twenty past eleven.

Was the priest a drunkard? I asked myself glancing at the empty bed in the alcove. Or was he one for whom the weight of the priesthood had proved too great a burden? Or was he, like so many of his fellow priests, woman-troubled? Whatever menace hung above him, he seemed to be holing up like a frightened animal.

Standing in the turret I looked out over the black clumps of rhododendron, over the face of the sea, past the cliffside pitted with seals' caves, past the cloven rock to the cluster of lights on the far shore. I remained there watching the lighthouse—once, twice, three times—splay its beam. Then I saw the seascape revert to darkness.

Tired after the day, I took off my clothes. Standing in midfloor, one ear turned towards the doorway, I flexed and exercised my naked body for a time. Then I pulled on my pyjamas and lay on the divan bed. Stretching myself with my fingers interlocked about my poll I looked up at the ceiling.

Had I pushed myself too far that day? Had I carried over into the act of driving the tension of my roadwork—that harsh grind of pushing my body closer to the ultimate boundary of its abilities? I rejected the idea. Last year, I reflected, I had missed winning the senior mile by a yard: this year, if the sports' writers were to be believed, O'Connell, the man who had beaten me then, was on the downgrade. I was already being hailed as the new champion —'a certain erratic brilliance notwithstanding,' one of the journalists had written. This year I told myself, God willing, or even with the devil's luck, I would beat O'Connell! And any others like O'Connell who thought they could run the mile. After that, national representation was open to me, followed possibly by an athletic scholarship to the United States. Names of places such as Tokyo, Hawaii, Auckland and Helsinki loomed up before me—I even saw myself on the Olympic team. All this if only I got the initial break of beating O'Connell.

Another side of my mind began to address my taut body, telling it that it would be happier lolling on a beach in Spain or France. There perhaps, a full-bosomed girl would touch my shoulder-blades with gentle fingertips. Why then endure such discipline? Why deny myself little luxuries? Did I always have to treat my trunk and limbs as instruments?

I sighed: for the last five of my twenty-two years, ever since I had won the event in the National Colleges Championships, I had been obsessed by the idea of winning the senior mile. While my sisters and brothers, who referred to me mockingly as 'the Miler', danced and drank, I lived under the tyranny of the stop-watch.

In the wan light of the bedroom I looked across at the priest's bed: perhaps he too had disciplined himself over-severely, until at last his nerves had sheered off track. Drawing in air slowly through my nostrils I tried to determine the physical appearance of the man. Fat or thin? Shivery or steady? Morose or loquacious? Semi-sane or downright crazy?

The smell told me nothing. The broad monastic bed in the alcove was altar-linen clean. I was tempted to rise and touch the priestly pillow and the clean blue coverlet: I did not do so, for I feared that with the fine attunement of his senses the priest might know that I had touched a part of him he held sacramental. 'Who's been sleeping in my bed?' I found myself saying, mimicking Baby Bear in the nursery story.

I blew out the candle flame. For a few moments, a spark on the wick trailed acrid smoke into the air of the room.

The divan was pleasantly hard. I rolled over on one side, turning my face to the wall. I recalled the ploughman (now probably as pleasantly tired as I was) and the old man on the pier cursing the breeding seals. I smiled wryly at the recollection of the trio of wanton tinker girls and finally sent my thoughts out from under the cloven stone to race over the sea and reach the light cluster on the far shore. Invariably a sound sleeper, I soon drifted off.

*   *   *

Asleep, and yet not fully so, I heard someone enter the room. A lightly-built man if I read his movements accurately. A non-smoker too, my keen sense of smell told me; on drowsy balance my mind was slow to rise consciously to the occasion so that I set aside the temptation to read other clues that came and went on the air of the bedroom. No whiskey, of that I was sure. Soap, such as I had used myself—he must have taken a late bath and—no smell of incense! I probed no more. Subconsciously I continued to sift him, and found neither enmity nor peril about him. I recorded a vague sense of inevitability about his coming as he moved lightly across the floor and stepped down to where his bed was. I heard him rise to tiptoe to draw across the curtain and vaguely realized that where he lay would be no more than seven or eight feet from me. I wondered if he snored. Again I heard the curtain rings bunch, stop, and ever so lightly creak across. After that, a last spark of my consciousness tried vainly to interpret the sounds of his clothes as he removed them: I should, by right, hear the muted crackle of his clerical collar and the rustle of the stock being folded in his hands. Too tired to sift the sounds further, I sank gently into sleep.

After a time (an hour? two hours?) I woke. My shoulder-blades felt cold. Groping, I found that the light upper quilt had slid to the floor. I heaved over and groped about on the floor to find it, at the same time being careful to make no sound that would disturb my room-mate. And then, as I twisted on the bed, the cramp struck!

Struck? Jesus! It did more than that! It zipped open the muscle of my right thigh, gripped whatever was sinewy between its iron fingertips, tied a knot in the thigh-string, pulled the ends tight and then zipped up the muscle again. The pain left me struggling, gasping, stretching, extending, butting, clawing, choking back obscenities, sweating, attempting to grip my thigh and later, when I dared to move, pummelling the bunched flesh. And at the moment when I thought the agony had eased, a second cramp unzipped the flesh of my other thigh, knotted up the thong of it and again zipped up the muscle. I blubbered, gibbered, extended both my legs to their full length in a vain effort to find relief by bracing the balls of my toes against the nonexistent end of the divan. With difficulty I held back a scream of rage and pain.

At last, as both cramps, having apparently passed the high point of their devilishness, eased for a moment, I gathered the bedclothes around my body, with the vague idea of bracing my foot-soles against something solid I rolled off the bed and on to the floor. There I lay gasping and grovelling as though I were emerging from an epileptic fit. For a moment or two the twin pains seemed static; yet it was as if the ferrule of an umbrella had been driven deep into the muscle of each of my thighs. Sweating profusely I lay without movement. Then I squirmed sidelong across the space that separated the priest's bed from mine. As I moved, the double cramp reached a new peak of agony. Unwittingly I clawed at the curtain above me so that the brass rod became dislodged and fell down, striking me on the shoulder before it clattered to the floor.

'Father!' I called. There was no sound from the bed beside me. Something told me that the priest was lying on his back staring up at the ceiling.

Stiffening my legs to the uttermost, and contorted with pain and anger, I raised myself on to my elbow and by a prodigious effort flung my arm across the priest's body. As I did so, my clawing fingers met the firm breasts of a woman.

The urgency of the pain in my underthighs more than offset my sense of discovery, so that once again my legs became rigid as they tried to outwit their tormentors. Stretch, stretch, stretch, lie doggo: ebb—ebb! I blubbered incoherently, as the knots grew less tight. Terrified even to stir, lest the contractions return to torture me, I lay there in dwindling agony.

At last . . . at last . . . A-a-ah! The devils were departing.

Exhausted but relieved, still swathed in bedclothes and with the curtain thrown awry across my body, I lay on the floor beside the bed. 'Mm,' I murmured sleepily. Dreamily I pulled the curtain and its entangled rod about my shoulders. The rod clanged a little and the curtain rings rattled. Breathing deeply I revelled in my release and soon fell asleep.

I do not know how long I slept. Opening my eyes I saw the first grey of day outside the slit of the turret window. A gust of wind thundered up from the sea and flung raindrops against the glass. I was now fully awake. My fingers, clutching as of their own accord, suddenly remembered.

I came carefully to my knees and looked down at the form in the bed below me. It seemed to lie in a foetal crouch. Its face was turned to the stone wall with the outer part of the bed offering me room. I paused for a full minute; then, a full-blooded shower urging me on, I raised the bedclothes and moved languorously in until my body came to where the bed had the warmth of an animal's lair. There I drew the bedcovers up about my shoulders. At first, I kept my body a little away from the woman, but later, studying every move before I made it, inch by inch I came closer. At last, I lay in a heap directly behind and against her. Seeking a signal from her body I waited.

At last she uttered a barely audible 'Mm,' then backed the minutest fraction towards me.

Then began the ritual of pleasure-movement. It resembled the fidgets of an athlete before the start of a race. At first each movement of mine was tentative and gentle, for I never knew the moment when the woman would spring up and rush out of the room. Then I found that my sense of timing, born of the racing mile, stood me in good stead. In my mind I went over the tactics demanded by the gun-lap, by the second lap and with a sense of zest looked forward to the task of knitting two good minutes to two minutes that were not so good. Experiencing something close to ecstasy I anticipated the moment when the bell would ring for the final lap and to the advent of the final sprint that would lead to victory—or defeat. And even as I visualized the flat rock in the cavern the woman swung easily to face me.

As I began to race this novel mile, further images—and roles —came and went in my mind. At one moment sea-water seemed to swirl about the rock, on which I, a grey bull seal, wrestled face to face with a young cow seal. Again, on a shift of fancy, I became the bright axe-head poised above the boulder, about to strike down into rock as it did in the legend of the giant in the far off past. Yet again, I was the ploughman on the hill flank, my ploughshare ripping the warm clay that faced the south and the sun. Again I held the live body of the idiot tinker girl in my arms: I even became the sinning priest of fiction, daring to break his vow of chastity and being broken himself thereby. But having taken these various roles, I reverted to being the miler, now running in the absolute certainty of victory and welcoming the sweat flowing down over his racing body. All the while I was acutely conscious that my imagination was affording me novel angles of vision on my movements so that my ecstasy was multiplied as would be a sensual act performed in a hall of mirrors.

The bell rang for the final lap. By now the woman had become my single remaining opponent. It was as if we two had outdistanced the field. For the first time in my racing life I was aware that my body and my imagination were working in harmony: my rival raced as if trying to convey the certainty that she would reach the line before I did. I imagined I saw on her constricted face a mocking smile that told me that once again I would become the ever-gallant second, the always-to-be-pitied, the rarely cherished of the commentators. But as we continued to race shoulder to shoulder I was again taken by the notion that the certainty of victory she appeared to convey was counterfeit, and that, with rare intuition, she was simulating this certainty so as to draw out the last ounce of my resources and ensure that no shred of strength would remain unused in my body or mind after we had finished the race.

As we raced round the last curve the roar of a thunder shower and the sound of the sea became the applause of a great crowd. I was conscious of the woman's limbs moving to a racing rhythm, one I found exhilarating beyond utterance and which complemented me fully. She was giving to the last yards of the race all the physical and imaginative resources she possessed so that with the finishing line drawing ever nearer she even dared to inch a little ahead of me. But my shoulder clung resolutely to hers and in the final few yards, when it seemed that I was beaten, I gathered the remnants of my frenzy, outsped her by the narrowest of margins, hurled myself forward and flung my body, and indeed my mind, upon the finishing line. Utterly spent, we collapsed, each on the other; as I gasped out to comfort her in defeat, by the wan light of morning I read in her wet eyes the implication that she construed her defeat as victory.

*　　*　　*

In the morning when I awoke, I found myself alone on the bed. I pulled on my track-suit, and later, having washed myself, went down to a breakfast of porridge, strong rashers, a large fried egg with the flavour of the sea in it, wholemeal bread and crabapple jelly. Of the mistress there was no sign.

I paid the red-faced maid what I owed, left the building, thumped my bag into the boot of the car, took the wheel, and for a moment looked up at the windows of the building. My gaze then shifted to glance up at the sign amid the fuchsias which read, 'Ave Maria: Guests Welcome'.

Why? I asked myself as, with gravel grinding under my tyres, I drove upwards to the roadway. For money? For release? For whim? For season? For no reason and for every reason? Why?

A final fleeting glance at the notice board showed me that it was mute and inscrutable: if it had been given a voice it would probably have answered, 'Such a foolish question!' With a look down at the pier, a stare at the pocked cliffs and the cloven headland and also with a muttered *'Mea culpa'* I drove off.

As I journeyed eastward, keeping the cliffs on my left hand, I knew that in the racing years ahead of me, whenever I heard the bell ringing to indicate the final lap of the mile, this woman would always be beside me, racing fluently on her tapered legs. And that, inexorably, I would wear her down, yard by yard, inch by inch, until with a final body thrust I would pass the line just ahead of her.

I also realized that this was the image that had hitherto been missing from my racing life: thus it was with a sense of elation that I drove onward, eager to find a suitable stretch of road where I could race and race, spurting towards the end in such a manner as would indicate the certainty of future victories.

My Love Has a Long Tail

The old man, a misty figure in a frayed overcoat, stood at a country crossroads on a morning in January. Behind him was a dripping clump of blackthorn bushes; below and around him were the rushy fields of a cutaway bog. Above his head were the underbellies of low clouds barely touched by the light of a sullen daybreak.

His cap vizor was drawn down over his small face which was dominated by askew steel-rimmed spectacles, one of the lenses of which, by the vice of being vertically cracked, made it sometimes appear that its owner had three eyes. At his knee, at the end of a loop of rusty chain, its neck encircled by a damp leather collar, its body scantily covered by a frayed dog-cover, stood a dispirited brindled and white greyhound.

From time to time the old man kept turning his face northward, to where the roadway emerged from among the grove of trees amid which the bland face of a 'great house' could barely be discerned.

Time passed. The mist had changed insidiously to fine rain. As the hound began to shiver and whine the old fellow stroked the animal's head, caress-covering its muzzle with a calloused hand. He began to mumble to himself with increasing loudness as if opposing unseen critics. He glanced back at the crouched cabin a few hundred yards away at the end of a torn passage into the bogland where lamplight showed wanly through a small recessed window. 'Why doesn't she go back to bed?' he said aloud. Then still louder, 'What has she to do now that I'm going to the Sales?' In a still louder tone, as if his wife could hear at that distance, 'Why the hell, woman, don't you go back to bed?' Then with an inconsequential snort, 'Yourself and your ten cartridges going out, to tally six birds and four cartridges comin' back!'

A donkey and cart loomed up behind him. The ironshod wheels of the cart had moved noiselessly on the bog-mould of the road surface so that they were beside him almost before he realized it. In the body of the cart stood a rusted milk-churn. A seated figure, its legs dangling, was hunched at the intersection of the shaft and floor of the vehicle.

'Any trace of a car to the north?' the waiting old man asked abruptly.

The sunken figure of the man on the cart, a dirty trenchcoat wrapped around him, slowly raised his head. 'Wee!' he said pulling on the reins. The donkey drew to a halt.

'That you, Mike?' he said in sham surprise.

'That's me, Peter! You're early for the creamery!'

'I thought I heard you . . . 'takin' stock',' the newcomer chuckled, obviously referring to Michael's habit of speaking to himself. He swung round as far as his cramped position would allow. 'No sign of a light to the north,' he said. 'If it passed Mr Hogan's you'd have seen it,' he added. Turning his head and looking down at the hound, 'You're off to the Sales?'

'I am.'

'You'll be expecting a tidy penny?'

'If breedin' counts he should sell well.'

'Three figures? Mebbe four?'

'If the Continentals attend, he could make any money.'

There was a pause as if for savouring this piece of information. Peering down at the hound, Peter asked, 'How's he bred?'

'He's by Soirée out of Full and Plenty.'

'Glover's bitch?'

'Aye.'

'The dam is good.'

'So is the sire.'

'What's his track name?'

'Parsley Sauce.'

'Damn good!' A faint teehee. After a pause, 'Does he have to run some class of a trial?'

'The trial is a matter of form. Buyers can size up a good hound by looks alone.'

'That's their trade! A good hound is better than a bawn of cows.' Meaningfully, 'But only if you're lucky.' Then to the donkey, 'Go on out! Tck-tck. Parsley Sauce,' Peter said with a chuckle as he drove on. 'Damn good.'

Mike was left alone in the misty rain. Looking after the donkey cart he muttered, then spat bitterly. Light began to sieve into the morning. From the high grove around Hogan's place a cock crowed. Rooks spoke hoarsely from a few desolate trees.

Mike thrust the crosspiece at the end of the chain-lead deep into his overcoat pocket. A drop gathered at the end of his nose. He opened his mouth once to reveal toothless gums. 'The bugger! With his Mr Hogan!' he said aloud. 'Everyone at the creamery'll know my business now.' The hound didn't look up at the sound of its owner's voice. A sidelong glance showed Mike that the lamplight no longer showed in the window of his cabin. On the ridge to the north a bright light showed in the yard of the 'great house'. Mike's head drooped: the hound's head dropped still lower. The chain noised so faintly that it seemed as if mist and rain had oiled it into silence. Mike could hear the rain dropping from the bushes behind him. There was the remote complaint of a morning bird.

At last the old man raised his head. He saw the reflection of headlights on the low clouds in the northern sky. Ah, here was the car topping the rise and moving through Hogan's Grove. The old man's face brightened. As he tugged on the chain the hound came dismally to life. 'My love has a long tail,' he said brightly as he waited for the car to draw up beside him.

The driver lowered the window and looked out. 'I'm to meet a man . . .' he began, and recognizing Mike and his hound blurted, 'Jesus!' Then with an explosive exclamation he made as if to drive off.

Michael clutched the edge of the car window. 'It's me, Mike Lanigan!' he shouted. ''Tis me, I tell you. Me you were to meet!'

The motor-car drew to a reluctant halt. Wearily the driver said, 'Too bloody well I know who it is. If I'd known it before now I'd have stayed at home in my warm bed.'

'You get my message, Tom?'

'You're too feckin' fly altogether,' the hackney driver said. 'You got a woman to phone from the store knowin' that if you phoned yourself I'd refuse you. "To meet a man at the Cross below Hogan's. A man who wanted to go on a drop run," he mimicked. 'Too well I know your drop run. Where the hell is it you wanted to go anyway?'

'To the Sales in Cork.'

'A three hours' run! Take your hand off the car. I've had my bellyful of you and your hounds at Trienafrinn coursing. Nearly got pneumonia loiterin' around and you blowin' your coal about all the great hounds you bred. My love has a long tail! My arse! Let go of the car, you whore's ghost, or I'll roll over you.'

'Damn it, man, you can't let me down.'

'I told you the last time that I was finished with you and your shaggin' hounds. It took me a solid week to wash the smell of that bloody snake out of my clean car. He all but pissed down on myself. Here, now, I warn you, take your hound out of the way or I won't be responsible for both o' you.'

'Tom! Wait! Blast it for a story, it means the world and all to me. The hound is listed in the Sales. His name is in print. Don't go! I'm two years feedin' him. Just for this day. If you seen all the cows' heads I boiled for him, all the dognuts he ate, all the bread Hannie baked for him. Red meat too! We left ourselves hungry to feed him. I'm a year walkin' him in weather good and bad. I lost money to the vet to put him right. If he misses today's Sales I'll have to sell out to Hogan. Tom, myself and your father were friends. You'll only be a few hours out, I promise you that. I'll pay you well. Before God, don't let me down.'

Wearily, the hackney driver slid the gear lever into neutral. In a tone of angry resignation he said, 'What money is in the Bank of Ireland won't pay me for the persecution I'm goin' to get from you today. I feel it in my bones. O Holy God!' he added impiously as he looked up into the agitated face outside his window. 'What time do you expect to be back?'

'We should be in Cork for ten o'clock. With a bit o' luck the dog'll be on the bench at eleven or half past. We should be back here for half past one at the very latest. The Continental buyers will be there. So I should get good money for him. Open the door in God's holy name.'

Tom beat his fist on the driving wheel. 'One condition!' he shouted. 'You'll sit on the back seat with your two arms around your hound. Keeping him up on your lap. He's not to touch the upholstery. I'm up to my neck in debt for the car.'

'Good man, Tom!'

'I know your couple of hours.'

'That I may be as dead as my father I'll make no delay.'

'An' you'll lob me thirty-four pounds into my hand. An'

guarantee to be back here for two o'clock at the latest.'

'I'll be back. But damn it for a story, Tom—thirty-four pounds! I haven't that much money in the world.'

'Watch your toes, I'm off!'

'Wait! Say thirty.'

'I won't say thirty. For thirty-three, ninety-nine. Are you goin' to piss or leave the pot?'

'Right! Let me sit in and not to have us standing here perished with the cold.'

'Us!' As he leaned back to open the door, the driver paused. 'If he pukes in the car, out ye go.'

Mike sat in the back seat, the hound cradled in his arms. His spectacles glinted in threefold light. The car door slammed shut. Glancing into the mirror the driver shouted, 'Don't attempt to raise that window. I don't care if the pair of ye freeze to death. And no smokin'.' He added ironically, 'My love has a long tail!' The car moved off.

The hackney driver was moonfaced with full lips and protruding eyes. He obviously lacked exercise. After a time Mike and himself struck up a semi-normal relationship. They chatted on deaths and weddings, on scandals, superstitions and unsolved murders. Now and again 'Don't touch that window!' the driver roared as Mike tried to take advantage of their quasi-friendship to sneak the window upwards.

Houses, villages, churches, pubs slid by in the as yet unreal light.

Now and then the greyhound whined his sense of discomfort. He even made frantic efforts to get off the knife edges of Mike's thighs; there ensued a confused flurry of arms and legs and paws in which the hound barely came off second best. Eventually the hound, resigned to his fate, sat on his perch panting and showing the purple and white insides of his mouth.

For the last twenty miles or so before entering the city the road was a series of S-hooks and horseshoe turns. The movements of the vehicle caused Mike and his hound to rock violently from side to side: there were times when the owner was sent sprawling sidelong against one or other of the doors. From time to time his lips moved either in pious prayer or picturesque obscenity.

On the outskirts of the city the emerging traffic of morning, much of it composed of heavy trucks and trailers, came thundering against them, threatening recurrently to squash the smaller vehicle as a clock-beetle is squashed under a midnight boot. The dog became agitated but Mike managed to hold on until at last before entering the city proper they saw the long palisade of corrugated iron which separated the greyhound track from the roadway. There was a great number of vehicles in the vicinity so that they were forced to park at some distance from the main gateway.

Once out of the car Mike snatched the old cover from the hound, took a folded and ironed one from the pocket of his overcoat, briskly shook it free, placed it on the back of his hound and tied its tapes around the neck and belly. From the driver's seat Tom eyed the cover with a merciless eye: it was obviously homemade, its bright yellow cloth trimmed in red with the letters ML, crudely cut from white cloth, still more crudely affixed to its right flank. The hound pricked up its ears on hearing the distant rattle whirr and whine of the electric hare, the baying of frustrated hounds, and the yells of partisans.

The enclosure was thronged with men and hounds. Huge countrymen in frieze overcoats wearing thick-soled boots clumped here and there in front of the stands, their bodies dwarfing the hounds they led. They moved towards the kennels according as their names were called to take part in the trials. When a trial was being run the waiting hounds became frenzied with excitement: once a large black hound, led by a girl of ten or so, slipped its collar, leaped the barricade and to the accompaniment of outraged shouts from the large throng of spectators took part in the race. Mike, no longer the disconsolate figure at the crossroads, suddenly became peremptory and authoritative. With a sharp word to the driver he disappeared into the crowd.

Tom sidled forward to lean against the rails bordering the track. There, he borrowed a sales list from a studious punter: he swore yet again on seeing Mike's hound was listed No. 135 —almost at the bottom of the card. He began to reckon what time it would be when he would get home. The trials already being run off in bunches of six hounds had begun at 9.30 and were due to end at 1.00 p.m. when there was a break for luncheon. That luncheon break would certainly not begin till 1.15 or 1.30; if he knew anything about the time-keeping of doggy men the sales proper wouldn't begin until a quarter to three. He now realized that Mike's hound wouldn't reach the sales table till seven or eight o'clock at night.

'The son of a bitch!' he muttered. 'Himself and his drop run. I'll be lucky if I get home by midnight.' He then went off to protest to his fare.

He found Mike, surrounded by his cronies, his spectacles agleam, a glass of porter in his hand, standing imperiously in the bar. Mike became supercilious when he saw the driver approaching. He was quite tolerant of Tom's attack. In his eye was the gleam of an amused gambler. He winked at his companions as if asking them to bear with him in this intrusion. But, narrowing his eyes, Tom noticed that the old fellow was in the company of town and city handlers and not among the well-dressed owners. The smallholder owner was a thing of the past, he told himself with some satisfaction.

Somewhat consoled by his conclusion, Tom returned to the enclosure where he looked around in search of the foreign buyers. He visualized them as wearing wine-coloured or beige leather jackets under camel-hair coats lined with pure wool, their splendour crowned by green velours hats with a blackcock's feather in the band. These were nowhere to be seen.

The hackney driver walked out through the main gateway and trundled to the nearest pub, which was about four or five hundred yards away. He was out of breath when he entered the empty lounge. He ordered a hot whiskey and sat back in resignation to face the wearisome day. Hannie would think he was out of his mind, he told himself, as the taste of hot whiskey, lemon and cloves pleasantly bit his tongue-tip. But where taking a phone message was concerned he had never met a woman who could take one right. He rehearsed his homecoming: 'Wouldn't you have the common sense to ask who was hiring the car? Eh? Or ask where they wanted to go? Eh? Or when they expected to be back? Eh? Is it too much to ask that whenever that bloody phone rings you should ask yourself "Who? When? Where? What? Why? and How much?" Eh?'

Much later he drained the dregs of the whiskey and returned to the track. 'Second last,' the punter at the rails said in answer to Tom's query as to how Parsley Sauce had fared in the trial.

*   *   *

56

At last there was movement in the enclosure. A triptych dais or desk, its front taller than its rear, had been placed in the stand nine or ten steps above the ground—this to accommodate the auctioneer, the relief auctioneer and the clerk. A low table was placed in front of this dais and three chairs set behind it—all with due solemnity. Microphone-testing over, three men advanced on the stand with the solemnity of priests entering a sanctuary. Taking his place behind the desk, the first auctioneer, his bald head glistening, his features wine-red as a consequence of a good luncheon, glared around him at the scattered crowd. He tapped his fingernails on the microphone, then as if in rage he struck the desk a resounding crack with his gavel. Instantly there was silence. All present poured out of the bar and gathered in a circle beneath the auctioneer.

Calling on the clerk to read the rules of the Sales, the auctioneer's voice roused echoes from the galvanized iron sheeting above his head. He frowned at the resonance of his own voice. The clerk began to read, quietly laying stress on the fact that as soon as he had placed his hound on the table in front of the dais each owner would whisper the reserve price to him, the clerk. This was important, he said, looking meekly down.

The assistant auctioneer retreated a step, and, with the volume adjusted, the auction proper began; the clerk's eyes as he read the bids were the darting eyes of a fox.

The Sales droned on and on. A jealous sigh went through the crowd as one hound made £2,800. About six o'clock the lights on the stand were turned on. There was now only a small knot of people left around the table. Beyond them the track seemed to extend endlessly and intimidatingly beyond the circle of wan light. Beyond the track the amber city lights glowed in aureoles of mist.

At last Tom heard Lot 135 being called. He left the rails and stood a little distance from the knot of people. He saw Mike crouching to lift the hound by its four legs and place it proudly on the table.

'Eight hundred and fifty,' Mike said in a whisper to the clerk. Writing the figure the clerk rolled his eyes incredulously. The small crowd tittered. Mike's lips twitched as, proudly, he stood aside.

'What am I bid for Lot 135? Parsley Sauce! A brindled and white two-year-old hound by Soirée out of Full and Plenty?'

The auctioneer went on to give the date the hound was whelped, its weight and the times of the races it had run.

Silence.

'Am I bid one hundred guineas for this son of a famous sire?'

Silence.

'Am I bid seventy-five guineas? Sixty guineas? Fifty guineas? Thirty guineas? Twenty-five, twenty-five, twenty-five—am I bid twenty-five guineas for this well-bred and well-proportioned hound?'

Silence.

'Gentlemen. Have I any bid at all? Final call, gentlemen. Any bid? No?'

Someone in the huddle sniggered. The gavel crashed down on the table. 'Take him down!' the auctioneer ordered peremptorily. Then 'Next lot, 136,' he said with a final look of disdain.

Mike gathered the hound's legs in his arms and turned away. The lights in the stand glittered crazily on the lenses of his glasses. He staggered down the steps. He carefully set the hound on the ground and walked away. After a few paces he took the old cover from underneath his overcoat and placed it on the hound's back. The hackney driver watched him as he tied the laces on the cover. He followed Mike as he walked towards the main gate. The old fellow seemed to have aged since morning. His lips were moving. Tom braced himself against weakness.

'Hey there, Mike,' he said hastening to catch up with him at the gate. 'How did things go?'

Mike never slackened his stride. 'You were watchin',' he said tonelessly.

The pair walked in silence towards where the car was parked. All the other cars had gone so that now it stood alone. 'Did you have a bite to eat?' the driver said.

'I had a drink.'

'It's a long fast,' the driver said. Mike did not reply.

As he opened the door of the car, 'I've a ground sheet in the boot,' Tom suggested. 'The hound can lie on it on the back seat. You can sit in front with myself.'

'I'll go as I came!'

They drove off. Now and again where amber street lights in the villages flickered in the car Tom glanced in the mirror and saw the frozen face of the old man, sitting erect with the hound spread awkwardly across his knees. The window was closed and a strong smell of kennel pervaded the vehicle. 'Smoke your pipe if you like,' Tom ventured.

'I won't bother,' the old man said sharply.

After travelling for some time Mike blurted, 'If you seen all the meat this fellah ate!'

'That a fact?'

'If I had a gun I'd shoot him.'

'That a fact?'

'We fed him like a gamecock. It cost us seven pounds a week to keep him. I went in debt for him.'

After a pause the old man's voice tailed off into inaudibility.

The driver sniffed. The smell of the car-heater, the smell of liniment, the smell of hot hound.

'Still an' all . . .' Mike began afresh.

'Eh?'

'If he got a fair crack o' the whip he'd have hammered the field. I know that in my heart. The favourite tried to savage him goin' in the wicket. I breed racers, not fighters. The man on the traps —he gave 'em a long slip—my fellah hates that. To cap everything he got a bump at the first bend and was crowded out at the last. Easy for the favourite to win when he had every dog cowarded before the race began.'

'That a fact?'

'If they ran them trials fair, there'd be five lengths of light between this lad and the rest of the field.'

'What about the Continentals?'

'The airport in Holland was closed with fog. The home crowd had the buyin' all to themselves. They had puffers drivin' up the prices for their chums. I wasn't the only one that was grumblin'.' A long pause.

They were passing through a village.

'Will you take a word of advice?' the driver asked.

'What is it?'

'Get out of hounds altogether!'

'You must be mad! How would you like it if I told you to get out of cars?'

'If you're rich an' you want to be poor, keep a horse, a hound and a whore.'

'Nonsense, man! Did you hear about O'Dea the ex-school-

59

master? Made six and a half thousand on his first hound. And what about the Mangan boy at the Lots whose dog sired the winner of the Irish Purse? Isn't he minting money out of the service. An' the woman in Oohashla who made a fortune out of one belly o' pups?'

'A middlin' hound is a curse from god.'

'A good hound is a gift of the Almighty.'

'A middlin' hound'd break Rockefeller.'

'A good hound is like winnin' the Sweepstake.'

'Take my advice! Forget your hounds!'

'I will not forget my hounds! You're a townie, so what do you know about the countryside at break o' day? The line of light in the east. The first stirring of the birds. We steppin' together, him and me. Muscle forming on his hindquarters as his body sheds fat. His motions those of a healthy hound. Then, when the time comes, there's the brace of hounds in slips. The hare goin' up the field. The hounds pullin' the slipper after them. Yeh, yeh, yeh! Who can whack that? Eh? Before I die I hope to own a hound that'll make the whole of Ireland ring with my name.'

'There's no affection to a hound.'

'The way his legs move are affection enough for me. My love has a long tail.'

They came to the crossroads where they had first met. Beyond the bogland was the small square of light in the window of the crouched cottage. Through the rookery trees, far above from Hogan's place, the yard light shone.

'What'll I be givin' you?' Mike asked.

'What we bargained for—thirty-four pounds.'

'You'll leave me without my supper.'

'Better you than me. You have your dream of Clounanna Altcar or Biscayne: I have my dream too—to educate six children.'

'What you're asking is out of all reason.'

'It's now ten o'clock at night. I'm with you since seven this morning. If I was paid by time 'twould cost you the most of a hundred quid. Wait'll I put on the roof light. Finger your fob like a good man. An' don't ask me for a luckpenny—that day is gone. That's it, thirty-three, thirty-four.' With a laugh, 'By right it should be guineas! Don't fall into the dyke. Slam the door easy.'

'Good luck whatever. Wait—if you're asked, say I refused good money.'

'I'll do that! Good luck, now. Don't forget—give up the shaggin' hounds.'

The car moved off leaving Mike alone in the drizzle and the dark. He stood irresolute for a moment or two. The bogland stretched for miles around him. As he began to rehearse aloud what he would say to his wife a figure materialized from behind a clump of furze on the roadside.

'Oaah, Mike!'—as if he had been waiting for a long time.

Grumpily, 'That you, Peter?'

Craftily, 'Aye.' A pause. 'Did you sell?'

'I could have sold, an' sold well. But I wasn't goin' to let him go at what was offered.'

'That was a tidy figure, I'd say?'

'Close to what I expected. But not the whole way.'

'You'll stick it out for the . . .' Peter put up four fingers.

'These buckoes took my name an' address. They have big cars. They'll likely be nosin' around here one of these days.'

'How did the trial go?'

'Trials are a matter of form. It's breedin' they judge by.'

'The Continentals?'

'Every class, creed an' denomination was there!'

'They'll give down the prices in the paper on Thursday. And the buyers too. Was that Tommy Dufficy was drivin' you?'

'It could have been one of the Dufficys, all right.'

'You're tired now. And hungry no doubt.'

'Tired? An' a new car under me? Hungry? An' lashin's of meat pies on the track?'

'What did he charge you for the car?'

'He'll make out the mileage, an' let me know when I'm in town.'

'My sister'll be wantin' him the day after tomorrow. A funeral in Tullabeg. I might travel myself. Parsley Sauce,' he muttered with a chuckle as he drifted away.

'The bastard!' Mike swore, having ensured that Peter was out of earshot. 'And a spy for Hogan! He's after sellin' his own holding, keepin' only a life interest. Now he wants every fox to have a burned tail like himself.'

The hound beside him, Mike squelched along the road towards the opening to the boggy passage that led to his cottage. 'Give up hounds!' he muttered, then raising his voice, 'My love has a long tail.' He stopped and fumbled in his pocket. 'One pound between me and pension day. I was to bring back tea, sugar and bread. Hannie'll have to do without. I'll have cold tongue for supper.' He laughed bitterly.

He walked a few steps, then came to a stop. Looking up in the direction of Hogan's he said, 'Big farmers gettin' bigger by the minute. I'd make money if I let my turf banks. But once in you couldn't get them out. I'll hold out as long as I can. I was sure the sale of the hound would tide me over till herself was of pension age. Then we'd be secure. My father lived through hard times. My grandfather was an evicted tenant. My great-grandfather weathered the Famine. We always lived close to the ground.'

He stood and looked around to ensure there was no one to hear. He raised his voice a little.

'Peasants they called us—the big bugs. But wars went over our heads. We lived where they died. We lived because we had the firin', the home bacon, the spuds, the fowl and the eggs. The milk too—even if it was goat's milk itself. Spring water, the rabbit, the hare, the salmon, the white trout, a handful of vegetables—maybe a few stools of rhubarb. I never attended a doctor in my life: we always had our own cures. Mebbe I should have gone to Birmingham like the rest. But I was sticky. I tried to escape by the short cut of the hound. Are there fellahs like me in other lands? In lands where the rain and puddle doesn't make them crazy like they make us here? Big bugs like Hogan waitin' to gobble up small lads like me. Castles fallin' and dung-hills risin'. The Troubles! All they signified was swappin' masters. Martin's store at the crossroads—I don't blame him for pressin' me for what I owe. He's on the way out too—the supermarkets in the towns are sucking him dry. Up to this I paid as I went. Now I'm in a hobble.'

He stood on the high road-edge. The wind whined. The dog whined. The bushes dripped.

'I'm not the only one is mad. All Europe is mad. The town market is gone. The fair is no more. The creamery is a thing of the past. A factory takes their place. All their eggs in one basket, an' if that basket falls what then—eh? Stone mad! If my Hannie sells six eggs to a house in town she's likely to get a process. If she dares sell a pound of home butter she's liable to end up in court. If she kills and draws a pullet and offers it to a customer she'll get a food prosecution. Is that madness?

Yes or no? Answer me!' His voice was loud now.

The wind. The whining of the hound. The drip of rain.

'If all goes to all the Council'll bury me.' After a pause his voice altered to self-pity. 'What am I now but a queer old fellah in the back seat of a car with a hound across my knees and lights flashin' on my face? I'm a class of a clown in a circus. An' yet, in spite of all, I'll hold to one creed till I go into the box. My love has a long tail! Take that from me and I'm no man. Let them jeer when they hear me sayin' it. My love has a long tail!' he shouted.

Craftily his voice lowered as again he began to mutter: 'Then again if I sold the hound well the pension officer might come down on Hannie when she applies. A peasant! What was Pope John but a peasant? Straight up out of the cowdung like myself. He had big ears like the old people I knew around here when I was young.'

Mike stood in reverie at the mouth of the tattered passage that led down to his cabin. He heard the mighty night with its fugitive stars assert itself around him. His senses probed it in a great ring, deciphering its minuscule noises, the antennae of his perceptions moving outwards, then swinging round the landscape almost in a complete circle. His nostrils flared as he inhaled the sulphurous odour of the black turf banks and the winter heather. There was a cry of a night-bird and the yelp of an animal in the dark; then from far down to the right came a mocking call of 'Cuckoo!' and again 'Cuckoo!'

That would be Peter, taunting him, Mike told himself quietly. Though his tormentor was surely half a mile away, he fancied he could see his leering face and his hand cupped about his mouth. The peasant was treacherous even where his fellow peasant was concerned. Mike could interpret the call. 'You're takin' stock,' it jeered, 'and now you have damn all to take stock of!' The call roused him to a slow anger. His mouth worked. His nostrils opened and closed.

'Peter, you bastard of a spy,' he jerked aloud as if the other could hear him, 'I'll best you yet.' Then turning to address others in an imaginary audience, 'You too, Hogan, bastard of a big farmer up there on the hill ready to gobble up my few acres. And you, bastard of a driver, Tom, that bled me white. Ye bastards at the track who put me last on the list. You bastard of an auctioneer and your penciller with the eyes of a fox. Ye bastards standin' around that gave no bid or that puffed when it suited. Ye bastards

63

from Amsterdam that never turned up. You bastard at the traps
with your long slip. You bastard at the store pressing me to pay.
Ye bastards in Brussels who won't let us live! Ye're nothing but
a pack of bastards, the lot of ye. But before the face o' Christ I'll
beat ye all yet!'

The cottage door dragged along the floor as it was being opened
from the inside. The dim square of light above the outside half-
door was flawed by the upper part of the body of a smallish
woman. Her head seemed permanently twisted to one side so that
the grey bun of hair on her poll could barely be discerned. Leaning
her forearms on the ledge of the half-door, she waited.

Mike braced himself. He lifted his small crowded face with its
glinting glasses. He wiped the froth from his mouth corners with
the back of his hand. Then, leading his hound, he squelched
across the quaking bridge of sods and bogdeal as he moved down
towards the crouched form of his waiting wife.

The Acolyte

The swing-doors leading from the side-entrance parted with a
thud and the little old woman, her bulging message bag weighing
her down, trundled into the bar. From the darkness behind her
came the sound of wind swirling up from the pier.

'You're wanted outside,' she growled.

The publican ceased swabbing the high counter. 'Who wants
me?' he asked.

'Who do you think?'

'Well, who do I think?'

'It's her!' As the little old woman reached the foot of the stairway
that led upwards from the bar she paused and looked uneasily
upwards. Setting down her message bag she glared sidelong at the
publican. 'If I was you I'd go out quick,' she added.

The publican looked steadily at the old woman. On his forehead
a bar of sweat glistened under the horizontal fluorescent light
above his head. His lower lip tightened over his upper lip, so that
when released the spiky grey-black hairs of his short moustache
bristled. He turned his head, framed as it was by the array of
coloured bottles ranked before a mirror, and glanced quickly at
the side-door through which the old servant had entered. Raising
his arm, he turned down the sound of a television set placed on a
shelf in an upper corner of the bar.

'What the hell does she want?' he blurted in a low voice.

'Why don't you ask *her*?' Noting how the publican glanced
anxiously at the stairway, the old woman added, 'Go on out: I'll
keep the missus in play.' As the man made angrily yet reluctantly
to move towards the side-door she added, 'Put on your jacket or
you'll catch your death. I'm minding you for forty-four years and
you're still a fool.'

The publican hesitated. Then, muttering as he turned, he lifted
his jacket from a coat hook on the wall at the end of the bar. As

on an afterthought, he took down a bunch of keys, glanced around at his shining bar-room, and went out the side-door. A gust of wind up from the harbour swirled sidelong into the archway and touched his shop-warm face.

In the comparative darkness outside, the man's eyes, accustomed to the brightness of the bar-room, failed at first to see the woman. Then he discerned her outline against the reflected light from the pavement outside and also against the faint glow that seemed to emanate from the triangular green that marked the heart of the town.

Her back set against the wall, the woman stood on the first edge of archway darkness. She was a low-sized woman in her late twenties or early thirties with a still girlish appearance. As, slowly, she turned her head towards him, her face became an olive oval, and the cream-coloured toggles of her dark duffle-coat shone in the shade. The archway smelled strongly of malt and salt, of urine, whitewash and tar.

In the street outside, wind, scattering grains of rain, gusted fiercely, then died.

'What is it?' the publican asked harshly. When the woman did not answer, 'I warned you not to come here,' he barked.

Still the woman did not reply. Her gaze swung outward towards the grassy space and the trim row of houses beyond it.

The man strode past her to the outer mouth of the archway. He glanced sharply up and down the rain-washed deserted street. Then he stalked backwards to the middle of the archway, passing the woman as he did so. He stood glaring at the amber-coloured opaque glass of the swing-doors. Addressing her sidelong, 'What do you want?'

'I want nothin',' the woman said quietly.

'What the hell are you doin' here so? I haven't all night. Customers'll be in soon. Out with it!'

The woman did not answer. The man was now standing about three or four feet from her and to one side. 'You're gettin' your money regular? Well?' he demanded.

'I want nothin', I tell you.' After a slight pause she added, 'It's him . . .'

'What about him?'

'He's eight now.'

'What if he is?'

'I seen you watchin' him at the Regatta.'

The man snorted in lieu of reply.

'He wants to go inside the altar,' the woman said quietly.

'The altar!' the man almost snarled. He paused as in puzzlement, then snorted in a way that ended in a short laugh. Abruptly, 'He can put it out of his head. And you likewise!'

The man swung towards the side-door in mock-finality. At the last moment he turned his lurch of departure into verifying that no one was coming out.

'I tried to get him to put it out of his head,' the woman said.

'You gave your word that you'd make no ins or outs on me!'

'Nor did I all these years. This is different.'

'What way is it different?'

'The boy won't give in. I went to Father Timoney.'

'You had no right to go to Father Timoney!'

'I had every right!'

'An' what did *he* say?'

'He said that he had taken on the complement of altar boys for this year. An' that next year was all booked up too.'

'That finishes it so!'

'It does not finish it . . .'

'Why so doesn't it?'

'The priest took on Dr Falvey's son after he had refused me!'

'Falvey's son, eh?' the publican said angrily but thoughtfully. He paused for a moment. 'Ah, for Christ's sake, woman, it's a thing of nothin'!'

'It means a great deal to me.'

'I'll buy him a bloody bicycle.'

'Keep your bicycle. I want him inside the rails.'

'What the hell do you expect *me* to do?'

'Father Timoney is a fair man. He knows how the land lies between me and you. 'Tisn't because he doesn't want a by-child inside the rails that he refused.'

'Why was it so?'

'He doesn't want it to trouble *you*.'

There was a short pause.

'I don't want him there and that's all there's to it!' the publican declared. 'Cocked up Sunday after Sunday for the parish to remark on him.'

The man paced agitatedly to the mouth of the archway. He

glanced furtively up and down the street, then returned to the side-door where the amber light touched his features. Taking out the bunch of keys as alibi he moved beyond the opening of the inner archway and paused before the closed door of the store. There he seemed to change his mind and again paced back towards the woman. As he was returning he glanced upwards at the lighted window of the kitchen overhead.

The woman watched him as with the patience of an understanding wife. When he had come close to her she said, 'If Father Timoney gets to know that you have no objection he'll let him in like a shot!'

'I'd like my job!'

'You could put it to the priest in a roundabout way.'

'What roundabout way?'

'Say that the altar boys are a credit to him. That you'd be proud to have anyone belongin' to you an altar boy. That it would be nice for a mother especially, to have a child so near to God. The priest will understand.'

'Count me out of it,' the publican said harshly. Rounding on the woman, 'You're goin' back on your word.'

'No one went back on his word but you!' the woman flashed. 'You swore that if anythin' happened you'd marry me. An' I only a servant girl on your floor. An' then you went off and married that dried-up craw-thumper upstairs!'

'Leave my wife out of this! If it's more money you want why don't you come out with it plump and plain?'

'Money! What bloody good is your money to you? An' you not havin' a chick or a child after you! No one but my Daniel.'

'That was more o' your blackguarding! Callin' him after my father.'

'I'll call him anything I like. I earned him hard. I'm not asking you to own up to him publicly. Only to let the boy go where he wants to go. An' give me and him some comfort in our lonesomeness.'

'Jesus, woman! What comfort?'

'You wouldn't understand. Whiskey, porter, wine, beer, kegs an' bottles, noggins and pints, that's all your mind can rise to. How could you be expected to know what comfort 'twould give me to see . . .'

'To see what?'

'To see his dark head under the raised chalice. To see him ringin' the consecration bell. To see him puttin' the gold plate under my chin at Communion time. To have the smell of incense off his clothes when he'd come home.'

'Is that all?' mock-tolerantly.

' 'Tis not all! To see him in his white surplice with the lace on it. And his red soutane. To watch him walkin' without sound on the tiles of the sanctuary. To see the light on his face an' he puttin' the taper to the candles. To see him carryin' the cross at the blessin' of a coffin. To see him holdin' the holy water bucket for the priest at the blessin' of the boats. On the day of the bishop too and at a wedding as well! At a weddin'—that's what I said,' the woman almost spat. 'And there's no one denyin' him all that but you. Him that for want of a few words between us at an altar rail would be the pride o' your barren life.'

The side-door to the bar opened and the old servant woman put out her head. 'Is that bitch gone?' she said, pretending not to see the younger woman. As the young woman flared up and came sharply away from the wall the publican pushed the old woman back into the bar. The swing-doors closed with a knock, a swish and a slam.

The hiss and clank of a bicycle were heard passing on the roadway. The publican retreated to the deeper darkness beyond the arch where plastic yellow crates were piled higgledy-piggledy against the wall. His back turned, he stood as if examining them.

When the sound of the passing cycle had fizzled away downhill the publican crossed the splay of light from the door panel and came close to the woman. 'Puttin' him inside the rails, 'tis yourself you're gratifyin',' he said with a sneer. 'And not me or your son!'

'*Our* son!'

'Your son and yours only! A bargain made and sealed by money and sweat!'

'No bargain can cancel blood!'

'Many a bargain can cancel blood. By thinkin' only of your fancies you don't give a God's curse how you daub me and the woman upstairs. An' maybe daub the boy most of all. For when he comes to manhood he'll ask you why did *you* destroy him? 'Tis you put the notion into his head and no one else. For spite you did it. And mark my words, in the heel of the hunt you'll daub yourself most of all . . .'

'I never drew it down to him. I can swear that on the cross o' Christ!'

'A woman has ways of gettin' her cracked ideas across without sayin' a word. I'll not go next nor near the priest. Off with you now!'

The man and the woman paused as the sound of footsteps came from the timber floor of the room overhead.

'Day or night I'll not rest,' said the woman with a menacing quiet, 'till I place him where I said. You hear me now!'

'Do your best!'

'I'll bullrag your name high an' low. I'll tell how you coaxed me into the top back room above. An' when you stole into our house below, how you had your ear cocked for my bed-ridden mother. I'll tell too how you offered me money to go to England.'

'I never offered you money to go anywhere.'

'Micksum Shea was your agent. You daren't deny it. He fell out with you afterwards. He can prove it up to the hilt. Don't push me too far, I warn you!'

The publican retreated a few steps. He turned and looked out at the white stones that edged the green. 'For God's sake, woman, take it easy,' he pleaded. 'I wish neither you nor him any harm. Is it a crime for a man to keep up appearances?'

'Appearances!' the woman shrilled.

'Easy now! Maybe as the years pass I'll do better for both of ye. What good are incense and candlelight? You can't eat nor drink nor wear faldals like that.'

'It's the only life left me.'

'Is it out of your mind you are?'

'Maybe I am. You have your shinin' shop and your customers, your house, your car, your summer lodge at the Point, your holiday in the Canaries. What have I? Sweet bugger-all except the single rearin' of my son. That an' the tendin' of my crippled mother. I have nothin', I tell you, except what I'm aimin' to win through him. An' what harm was it if I put it into his head in my woman's way? Is that a crime?'

'While ago you were denyin' it on the cross o' Christ. What is your word worth?'

'It's the word of an addled woman, that's all.'

There was a period of irresolute calm. The calm had a measure of desperation to it. It was as if each of the protagonists was vaguely trying to accommodate the other. The woman, her back set resolutely against the wall of the archway, stared across at the ball-stippled wall facing her.

'When you're on your own,' she said sadly, 'things take over your mind. And I must give in to this fancy or be destroyed. If the boy goes inside the altar, each passing day will mean a lot to me. Good Friday, Easter Sunday, the Feast of the Immaculate Conception or Christmas Day—I'll have a new way of lookin' at them. If I was washing out the hall for the bank manager's wife and if I heard the church bell ringing, I could lean back on the calves of my legs and think of him bringing the key of the tabernacle to the priest. If I saw the children dressed for the May procession I'd think of him strewing rose petals before the Host. I'd give anythin' to coax you to my way of thinkin'. I'd even . . .' her faltering voice broke off.

'You'd even what?'

'I'd even let you have me like you had me before,' she said in a blotched tone of voice, 'and take my chance again although I know all the trouble it brought me already. An' I say that knowin' that I'm suggestin' wrong. But I also say it knowin' that I never let anyone near me except yourself. That's how strong I feel about it. An' may God forgive me my sins.'

The publican said nothing. His features became twisted. He gulped. His eyes appeared to grow larger. He looked this way and that. An empty canister rolling on the roadway outside roused him. He plodded dully towards the store, turned the key in the lock, switched on the light inside the door and, after looking for a moment or two at the interior, he switched off the light, closed the door, locked it and walked slowly towards the side-door that led to the bar. His barely lighted face twitched in a remote understanding.

Just then the swing-doors opened suddenly and the old servant woman stuck out her head. 'Quick!' she said. 'She's gone out the front door.' The publican hurriedly brushed past her and barged into the bar.

On hearing the faint sound of footsteps in the street outside, the woman in the archway turned towards the wall, drew the hood of her duffle-coat over her head and bunched up her body with her back towards the street. The canister rattled merrily, remotely, downhill.

After a few moments the tall thin figure of a woman wearing a hat and dressed in black moved across the opening of the archway. A silver-mounted grey-furred claw brooch gleamed on her white blouse. Midway across the opening she paused, using the excuse of drawing on her gloves to let her eyes slide sideways to penetrate the archway gloom. After a while, her gloves apparently donned and smoothed to her satisfaction, 'Are you there, Nan?' she called out softly.

There was no reply from the archway. 'Come along, girl,' the publican's wife said. There was a pause, then the younger woman walked slowly out.

'I'll be with you as far as Egan's Lane,' the publican's wife said. 'I like to be early for Mass on a First Friday.'

In silence the pair moved down towards the church on the sea front. Walking on the inside of the pavement the younger woman was conscious of the high heels, the gilt prayer book, the silver-mounted brooch, the gloves and the tall fall of the coat that elongated the figure of the publican's wife. The rain spat erratically and the wind gusted wanly about them. Pavement and roadway glistened. Reflected lights were barely discernible on the water of the small harbour below.

After a walk for a little distance, 'You were speaking to the Boss?' the older woman said.

'Yes, m'm.'

'Something you wanted?' When the younger woman did not reply, the older woman added quietly, 'I need to know.'

'I wanted to put David inside the altar.'

'The Boss fussed, didn't he?'

'Yes, m'm.'

'Who's in charge of the altar boys—Father Timoney?'

'Yes, m'm.'

The woman tilted her head upwards on her long neck. 'Shouldn't be much difficulty about that! I'll see Father Timoney, myself.'

They walked along for a few steps. Then, 'You'll need a surplice and a soutane?'

'I have 'em, ma'am.'

'Slippers?'

'I have slippers too.'

'Good!' the publican's wife sighed. She looked down into the distant harbour. 'For the first time in my life I almost forgot the First Friday. I always like to be in church with ten minutes to spare, to see after the flowers on the altar and things like that. How's your mother?'

'Same way, m'm.'

'Still keeping to the bed?'

'Yes.'

'The weather is against her. Winter came in early this year. Here we are at Egan's Lane. Makes a short cut for you, doesn't it?'

'It does, m'm.'

'If you need anything like that again, won't you come to me first?'

'I will, m'm.'

After a pause: 'He's eight now, isn't he?'

'Going on nine, m'm.'

'Time passes so quickly.' Then as if groping to recall some half-forgotten matter, she said with the pretence of discovery, 'There's just one thing. Father Dan, the Boss's brother, comes home from Nevada every year in August. He often says Mass on Sundays in the parish church.'

'My Daniel spends August at my brother's place in the country.'

'Does he?'

'He gives a hand drawing home the turf.'

'Ah!' There was another thoughtful pause, preparatory to moving off downstreet. Then, with a conspiratorial smile, 'About the boy's going to the country in August, let that be confidential between us, eh?'

'Very well, m'm.'

'There are times when men need to be taught a lesson,' the older woman said with what appeared to be mock-severity. Then, her gloved fingers caressing the claw brooch, she added, as if addressing the lower apex of the green, 'Old retainers too!'

'Yes, m'm.'

'Off I go now. I never did like going into evening Mass at the last moment.'

The publican's wife went mincingly downstreet towards the church. As the wind rose, the canister accompanied her for a short distance, rolling and rattling along the edge of the roadway. Then, unexpectedly, it switched direction and came to a halt at the kerbside. The street was suddenly silent.

After having gone a little way down the laneway, the younger woman stopped. Setting her shoulderblades against an outhouse wall, she looked up at the sky. A sliver of moon rode calmly behind a moving screen of tattered clouds. The hood had slid backwards from her head so that her face remotely reflected the scudding pattern of the night heavens. Her eyes closed, her lips tightened and thinned, then began to writhe about her teeth. She murmured incoherently and began to swing her head from side to side. Suddenly the young woman's eyes sprang wide open. As on a vague realization she came away from the wall and hurried back to the mouth of the laneway above. Standing there she watched the publican's wife as she prepared to cross the roadway to the gateway of the church.

From the front doorway of the public-house the old servant woman had been watching both women. She had already seen them walk together as far as the laneway. She had seen them part. Only for a moment had her attention been distracted—this was by the rolling and rattling and glistening of the canister. She had recovered from this minute interruption in time to see the younger woman reappear at the opening of the laneway. She continued to watch as her mistress continued her stately journey to the church.

The old servant woman wore an overlong brown cardigan, the ends of which were crossed over her bosom and tucked inside the waistband of her black skirt. Though her arms were short, she insisted on clasping her hands behind her back. From time to time she allowed her small head to protrude at a point lower in the doorway than an observer would expect. The little head, when it emerged, was rendered still smaller by the beetling fascia board above her that hooded the shop windows and the archway. The faint light filtering through the opaque glass panels of the swing-doors just behind her brushed her shoulders and her wizened hair-coil with an amber glow.

Her manner of watching betrayed her country origins and conveyed a long tradition of being on the alert for police, bailiffs, excise officers, informers, agents and trouble-makers of many kinds. It also conveyed a sense of ancient loyalty together with the intuitive ability to follow the gist of a distant conversation and accurately interpret mental attitudes gleaned from gait, posture, pace, pause and head movements. From time to time the old woman glanced back over her shoulder to observe the thin vertical slice of her master which she could descry through the aperture left beween the not fully closed door-leaves behind her. This downward section, inadequate as it was, bisected the reflected light on the man's forehead, cut through the lower lip yet not quite mastering the spiky hairs of his moustache, and slit downwards over knuckles stilled in the act of swabbing. Moving her eyes back to the level of his face and shifting her gaze a fraction to left and right allowed her to recognize the glint of fear in the publican's eyes.

So engrossed in her watching was the servant woman that she failed to see the figure of an old man slowly crossing the road at the upper end of the town. One shoe on the kerb, he stood; his mouth falling loosely open, he remained motionless, watching through steel-rimmed thick-lensed glasses each of the three women in turn. He wore a heavy shabby overcoat which muffled up his body and throat leaving the pupils of his eyes the only part of him alive under the greasy vizor of his cap.

Having appraised the situation he moved cautiously on to the pavement, and, keeping close to the walls of the closed shops, he shuffled purposefully forward, keeping his gaze fixed on the movements of the women. He too appeared to have the ability to interpret their every movement and in some indefinable way, possibly by the thick licking of his lips when he observed the watcher in the public-house doorway throwing a half glance over her shoulder, conveyed his knowledge of the fourth watcher behind the bar counter. Stalking slowly forward he took in every detail of the scene, timing his approach to coincide with the downstreet disappearance of the two women.

He was almost upon her when the old servant woman turned her head and saw him. She made as if to flee indoors but the sound of the old fellow rasping harshly in his throat forced her to stand her ground. At the last moment she moved before him into the bar allowing one leaf of the swing-doors to bang almost into his face. He seemed to have anticipated this, for he caught it just in time and, wheezing tolerantly, entered the bar-room on her heels. At the foot of the stairs she turned her head slightly and flashed a warning at the waiting publican. 'Brr!' the old fellow said again, indicating that he had caught her redhanded. As both the servant woman and the publican looked at his face to verify this the old fellow stood still, his tongue heavy on his lower lip as if relishing the situation. To the two watchers the magnified pupils of his eyes, as seen through the lenses, were those of an all-seeing god.

In the street outside the rain had ceased. The wind made a vain effort to move the canister. The rain-polished surface of the roadway glinted at intervals all the way down to the church; there, as the last worshipper whisked inside the doorway, the bell in the stumpy steeple clanged rustily. In the little harbour the highriding huddle of trawlers indicated that the tide was almost full. The final pier light reflected on the moving surface of the water swirled in such a manner as suggested a swung thurible. It also vouched for deep waters far below.

A Lover of France

I

Due to a mistake on the part of the travel agent, the newly-married couple found themselves booked into separate cabins on the ferry boat to France.

Mary, as befitted a former nun, accepted the fact demurely; Joe, her husband of just ten hours, his bald head shining, his jaw jutting, seemed determined to make it clear at the purser's office that he had definitely contracted for a cabin for two on this, his wedding night.

The purser was urbane. He kept looking at the others in the queue and murmuring that Msieu could take up the matter with the travel agent on his return to Ireland. And if a refund were due to Msieu, it would certainly be made. He suggested that Msieu should share a cabin with some of the waiting gentlemen, otherwise . . . The purser then made the vague gesture of sleeping on the floor of the lounge. Joe turned aside to have a word with Mary: her flushed cheek and the gentle movement of her hands indicated that she didn't mind. As he turned back to accept, Joe's expression indicated that he thought it damned unfair.

*　　*　　*

After leaving the convent, the farewell tears of her companion nuns still stinging her cheeks, Mary Lavelle had spent some months in the back room of her widowed mother's cottage, emerging only in the winter darkness of Sunday mornings to attend early Mass in the village church. Alone in her cold covert, she excused her solitary existence by telling her mother—and herself —that she needed time 'to think things out'. Now and again, when the cottage was empty, she looked into her small mirror and, whimsically recalling a question from her childhood, asked her reflection, 'How now, brown cow?'

When time had passed without a decision being made, Mary's up-country aunt, an unmarried midwife, arrived and took control of the situation.

'She needs a man!' the aunt told her widowed sister in a hoarse whisper.

The mother mumbled in resignation as her sister went off to consult old cronies. Back again at nightfall, a smell of sherry from her breath, the midwife drew up a chair to her sister's side. After a glance at the bedroom door she whispered, 'Joe Hendron of Teercallaghan!'

The mother's head turned slowly. Her eyes were wide. 'The fellah that keeps the stallion?'

'The same! Well able to handle shy mares.'

'He's as old as a field!'

'In his mid-forties. Mary, with her thirty-one, is no chicken.'

'I met him once when Jim, God rest him, was alive. He never stopped talking about Napoleon and the Empress Josephine.'

'Nothing wrong with talkin' about France. Along with the sire horse he has a tidy little farm. No one in the place but himself.'

'Him with his check jacket and his riding britches. He'll drive her mad in a month.'

'She'll be mad in less if she isn't served! Not a syllable till I'm ready!'

The mother took out her rosary, blessed herself with the crucifix, kissed it and began to intone the Apostles' Creed.

Harried by her aunt, Mary emerged from seclusion to attend the Countrymen's Dinner and Social held annually in the Arms Hotel of the nearby town. Minor intrigue ensured that the aunt was seated beside Joe Hendron with her niece seated on her other side. When the company rose to intone grace, the aunt, with a glance across the table at a confederate, adroitly exchanged places with her niece. Joe, dressed in a navy-blue suit and a white shirt with a red tie, was pleased when one of the guests reminded him that he was wearing the colours of France. Later in the meal when the Beaujolais began to make him mellow Joe raised his glass and, taking care that his gold-topped bicuspid was seen, said, 'To the home of liberty and culture.' The toast drunk, Joe declared, 'If ever I marry, I'll spend my honeymoon in France!'

The crony across the table leaned forward and said, 'If I was as good-looking as Mary Lavelle there, I'd take you up on that, Joe Hendron.'

Mary's face with its small mole on one cheek burned a deeper olive; Joe leaned back in his chair to survey his table companion in a new light. Those nearest the pair, scenting game, chimed in.

It was a short campaign. The stallion-owner and the former nun were married with as much, and as little, ceremony as was considered suitable under the circumstances.

Dressed in her pale blue best the aunt preened herself as, the wedding breakfast over, the dusty mini-car, its exhaust-pipe shuddering and belching purple fume, with worn boots and tin cans clattering along the road behind it and a volcano kettle rattling among the worn suitcases in its boot, disappeared round a bend in the road.

In the vehicle Mary plucked a speck of confetti from a fold in her sleeve and then carefully dropped it on the cluttered ash-tray below the dashboard. She then resumed her watching of the road unwinding before her.

2

On the quay at Le Havre, seated squarely behind the steering wheel, his freshly shaved jaw gleaming blue, Joe spat into the palm of his hand and drove into the broader streets of the city.

Stallholders in midroad jeered at the sight of the rusty vehicle, its exhaust-pipe cannonading, its final old boot bouncing off the cobbles. Mary's ears began to burn: Joe seemed to relish the attention they were accorded.

As they moved into the countryside south of the city the bride of a day and a night bent her head over the map and did her best to find the next town on their journey southward to Paris. Joe began to hum 'The Marseillaise', now and again beating time on the steering wheel with his fist. His high spirits temporarily deserted him when, having decided to leave the autoroute, and having presented the card he had previously accepted at a tollgate, a vast amount of francs was demanded of him. There was also the patronizing sneer of a filling station attendant. Joe banished these reverses with a smile as if to convey 'We're here! In France! My life-long ambition is fulfilled! Nothing else matters!'

About midday they stopped at a seedy layby. In the adjoining restaurant Mary bought a *baguette*, cheese, cooked sausages and some saffron-coloured buns. Joe filled the volcano kettle with water in a nearby *lavabo*. Kneeling on the clay beside a settle in a clearing of scrub he stuffed the central chimney of the kettle with pieces of cardboard and twigs. Whistling confidently he set a match to the fuel. For Joe, boiling water in this utensil in the bogland at home was a simple matter: a small flame fed with pieces of dry turf and slivers of bogdeal and the water bubbled up in no time at all. But in this scabby roadside grove north of Paris, fuelled with material that was fire-resistant, the chimney spewed up palls of black smoke. From behind the bushes came coughs of protest.

Mary, seated on the grey plank of the settle, the food and delph spread on serviettes before her, looked down in silence as Joe's outpursed lips blew on the stubborn kettle. She was about to offer a word of caution when the chimney burst into flames. Then, seated on the settle opposite his wife, Joe munched contentedly. Food had never tasted better, he declared. Over the rim of her teacup Mary's eyes were on his grimy fingernails.

*   *   *

In Paris they stayed at a tall narrow hotel on one of the avenues radiating from the Arc de Triomphe. The August heat was stifling: their bedroom was on the top floor. There was no lift. Daring to open the French window of the room and take a single step forward into the crow's-nest of the balcony, Mary looked down and saw the traffic below appear as toys. Taken by a remote sense of vertigo she withdrew at once.

There were two beds in the room—a double bed and a single. The little bathroom had a shower and a bidet. Joe smirkingly conveyed that he knew what the bidet was for; demurely dropping her eyes Mary indicated that she already knew. They ate in the open at a café round the corner: Joe exchanged banter with the waiter in deplorable French while Mary continued to examine the large *carte*. Under the amber lights the meadow-yellow skin of Joe's face appeared a ghostly green.

Wearing only her long white cotton nightdress, Mary knelt on the floor beside the marriage bed. Her fingertips joined beneath her lowered head, her eyes closed, her lips moving silently, she prayed. Two slender braids of blonde brown hair were entwined at the nape of her neck. After a pause, Joe in striped flannelette pyjamas, knelt beside her: he wore cream-coloured woollen bedsocks the soles of which had turned brown with usage. Before Mary came to her feet her thumbnail made the triple sign of the Cross—on her forehead, mouth and between her breasts. Fleetingly, as she rose, her eyes circled the red velvet wallpaper of the shabby room.

She lay on the double bed half on her back, half on her side, her eyes fixed on the wall. Waiting, she stole her feet upward as if to avoid a later contact with the bedsocks. Joe's initial attempts at lovemaking were rhythmless. He sweated profusely. She got him to sidle out of the culmination; a nunnish murmur reminded him that he had slept badly on the boat and that there was a lifetime before them. Through the darkness traffic below hissed and growled mutedly.

The Louvre (entry free on Sundays!), Sacré Coeur (its ethereal perch touched Mary on a spiritual level), Montmartre (its women brashly touting sales for the artist lovers), a melon which they shared at a handcart in Ile de la Cité (seeds floating down over Joe's chin made him appear a greedy and grubby boy), the wine which Mary was lured into drinking with the evening meal (she then discovered a new note to her own laughter)—all fused to form a rather notable day.

The wine made Joe resolute: that night he took her as befitted the owner of a sire horse. Mary was as passive and as dutiful in the marriage act as once she had been in the office of her former vocation. Later, as he snored loudly, she lay awake, her eyes fixed on the ceiling of the room with its moving fans of light reflected from the boulevard below.

3

They left Paris and headed south. As they drove along, Joe managed to transfer to her some of the excitement he anticipated on seeing the Mediterranean and the Pyrenees for the first time. Mary got the impression that the car engine was running more coarsely than before, but then, she told herself, she knew nothing about combustion engines. At noon, halted in a shady layby, he proved quite adept at boiling the kettle so the pair enjoyed a tolerable meal of dark bread, cheese and sausages: later, Mary produced fruit and confectionery which she had held in womanly reserve. The meal over, Joe stretched full length on the grass in the shadow of a tree. Looking down on him as he slept, Mary's eyes softened as she watched the vulnerable expression on his face.

Lyons was a nightmare. The chaos of late afternoon traffic together with the sight of the raised baton of a gendarme on point duty filled Mary with something akin to fear. Joe, shouting joyously through the open window of the threadbare vehicle, pushed through the city centre and into the open countryside to the south. Late afternoon found them in a small town smelling of cigars and sewage. As dusk gathered, a ruined Roman temple, floodlit in rose pink, stood out against a dark hillside. Searching for a room, the word *'Complet'* met them everywhere. They slept badly, huddled together in the car.

Near Sète they came upon the Mediterranean for the first time. The harbour stank of fish. Joe insisted on bathing from a dark-sand beach on the edge of a town which did not appear on their map. His out-of-date swimming costume—it looped over his shoulders and had oval kidney vents—had, with age, bleached from navy-blue to a patchy purple. The legs of the costume extended downwards almost to his knees. His pale skin contrasted with the tan of the middle-aged women who, standing waist-deep in the waveless water, rested their fingertips on their hips and looked in disbelief from Joe to their menfolk on the beach and back again. Joe ventured to splash one of the women but she swivelled her head in disdain. From where she was seated in the car Mary could see the winks and nods that followed. Emerging from the water, Joe raced bonily up and down so as to dry himself. Back in the vehicle, despite the oppressive heat of the day, goose-pimples showed on his skin. From a seam in the costume he extracted a small pink comb and combed his sidelocks. Resuming the journey he seemed refreshed and happy. She need not worry, he told Mary, presently where France and Spain met, they would find an unspoiled fishing village where they would eat shellfish, drink Muscatel and bathe from golden sands.

Among the villages west of Bezair they were forced to spend a second night in the car. Pushing south along minor roads they

moved through trembling heat over a baking landscape defined
only by cypress trees, black pillars of ill-omen looming upwards
through the pulsing air. Her fingers damp on the map, Mary
guessed that, by now, they had skirted Narbonne and, keeping the
sea to their left hand, were facing rather erratically for Perpignan
beyond which they could already see, pencilled in diminishing
progression, the outlines of the French Pyrenees.

*   *   *

It was now late afternoon. The merged bulk of landscape and
skyscape began to glow at its edges so that it resembled a banked
coalfire. To the southwest and west the mountain ranges had
receded into a pepper-coloured gauze with dark elements of blue
at its core. The immediate landscape was lowlying and featureless.
Lightning blinked and was gone, but not before it left on the dim
world the memory of a colour like that of pale white wine. The
air grew ominously cooler. The engine of the car began to rattle.
Joe, peering to scout the way ahead, clamped his foot down on
the accelerator: with every revolution that followed the din became
more strident. Suddenly the engine stopped, was restarted and,
having jerked fitfully forward for fifty yards or so, cut out completely. The vehicle had now come to a halt with its off front
wheel sunk in a shallow ditch by the side of the narrow road.
    The pair looked out at the darkening world. Willows and
bamboos formed a fence on either side of the road; between the
slats of the fence could be seen the unreal green of vine leaves
and the menacing purple of clustered grapes. Joe and Mary sat
immobile as immense panes of light came and went on the phantom
uplands. They heard the faraway cannonading of thunder. Blobs
of rain stippled the windshield. Presently the downpour, beating
on the roof and bonnet of the car, resembled the sound made by
a crazy kettle-drummer. Burrum-burrum went the rain, delving,
throbbing, pelting, sounding and resounding as it pounded on the
vehicle and pocked the surface of the road. The roof began to
leak. Lightning and thunder redoubled in brilliance and reverber-
ation; the spades of the rain dug into the roadway until the road
itself took on the appearance of a brown stream hastening and
hissing in many directions. Yet again splash and burrum, creating
a mist of impact and evaporation as blink and explosion alternated

83

in the mountain peaks. There was a smell of sulphur in the air. Water seeped in under the doors of the car so that Joe and Mary had to raise their shoes from the floor.

Unexpectedly, the rain ceased. The couple peered out through the misted glass. A cessation or an end? Dared they venture out? Dared they remain longer in the car? Would their belongings be stolen if left unattended? If they *did* find a house in this sodden landscape how would they be received?

After a time, shoes and stockings in hand, his trouser-ends rolled up above his knees, Joe left the car and began to trudge-wade along the road to the south.

'Wait!' Mary cried as, barefooted, she splashed after him. The ebbing flood still hissed between the stems of the low fence. Mirrored in Mary's upward glance was the fear that darkness would soon encircle them in a hostile unknown. They splashed along: around them lay a spread of lowlying land holding seething lakes of water.

Suddenly, with a flash more brilliant than its fellows followed by an immediate salvo of thunderguns, the deluge began afresh. They stood together, crouching a little, allowing the monstrous sky to have its way with them. Soon they were drenched. The dark cypresses of the near horizon were barely discernible. Still the pair stood in a world of squelch, splash and hiss. The gold of lightning came and went in the blue and pepper of the dim Pyrenees. Burrum, drum, and again the hiss and roar of water scourged and scourging.

Mary's hair had darkened in the rain. It clung to her skull. The sopping ends of her dress swirled in the water. She looked up at the tyrant sky, then glared at the uncomprehending man beside her. She opened her mouth and with a cry quartered by fear, rage, frustration and discomfort staggered towards the roadside. There, raising her fists above her head, she thumped down full length on a lump of earth the top of which showed above the level of the flood. Her fists began to beat earth and water, her open mouth dug into the steaming clay, while her bare toes did their best to beat a tattoo on the deeper water behind her.

Suddenly protective, Joe bent over her. He seemed uncertain whether his touch would infuriate or calm her. He watched the flurry of her white feet and listened to her open-mouthed cries of outrage and despair. As the din of the thunderstorm continued, her wails grew more abandoned. Reaching a peak they cut off abruptly as a steady swish of displaced water was heard. As if attentive to this new sound the rain ceased. Mary raised her head to listen.

4

A long shabby motor-car approached casting aside two gull-wings of water as it came. Joe flapped his arms to indicate where Mary was lying. As it slowed down a wave of water broke over the recumbent figure of Mary. A woman leaned sideways from behind the steering wheel, lowered the window, and called out in a cultured English voice, 'What's the matter?' Bleakly Joe indicated his prone wife.

The driver, whose hair was quite blue and whose elderly face was dotted with wens and criss-crossed with wrinkles, looked down at Mary. Then she crowed like a cock. Mary turned her head at the sound.

'Gipsies?' the newcomer shouted.

'No, ma'am, we're not gipsies,' Joe said.

'Have you got a car?'

Joe indicated the direction from which they had come.

As if speaking to herself the woman said, 'Can't leave them here.' Then, directly, 'Sit in, the pair of you! Never mind your wet clothes! Come along.'

As Mary got ruefully to her feet, her wet clothes moulding her firm body, the newcomer again crowed loudly.

Joe took his seat in the back of the vehicle; murmuring apologies for the condition of her clothes, Mary sat beside the driver. They rode along in comparative silence, the woman concentrating on holding to the middle of the flooded road. Arrived at the place where the little car was ditched, the driver crowed her disbelief. 'Take your possessions out of that wretched mousetrap! Push it farther into the fence,' she commanded. Later, as Joe, carrying the fibre suitcases returned to the larger car, the volcano kettle, which was strapped to one of the cases, banged off the door of the car, earning a cluck of disapproval from the woman. Presently, as they drove along on higher ground, there was only a thin film of

85

water on the road surface; later still the roadway showed no signs of rain having fallen.

The fan of the car-heater blew warm air between Mary's thighs. She drew strands of drenched hair back over her ears. The old freckled fingers on the steering wheel were encrusted with silver rings: many of these were of Red Indian design and had stones of veined turquoise. As Mary's eyes were sidelong on these rings the woman shot a quick downward glance in her direction: Mary reacted by covering the fingers of her left hand. 'Honeymooners?' the woman enquired with a chuckle. Mary responded with a barely audible 'Yes'.

It was now dusk. To the east a shimmer showed on the surface of the sea. A headland bulked between them and the north. The car skirted a village, crossed a causeway, zig-zagged upwards over a shale road and, as the driver wrestled with the wheel, picket fences, villa walls and balconies swung about in a series of demented semicircles. At last the car came to a heavy halt beside the door of a garage.

The opened door of the villa led to a spacious L-shaped room. There was a smell of wine and cigarillos. When the light was switched on, a sleepy borzoi came out to greet them. 'Good dog, Nikolai!' the woman said. Then over her shoulder, 'I'm Lady Margaret.' Placing her face close to the dog's head she crowed affectionately.

A bath, dry clothes and later a candlelit meal on the balcony. Faraway the splayed beam of a lighthouse came and went.

Joe and Mary remained in the villa for the night. There was no sense of unease about the morning meal. 'Where in heaven's name do you propose going?' Lady Margaret's question forestalled their making a decision. 'Chores to be done here. I'm too old for the garden.' When it became clear that they were welcome the pair stayed on.

With each day that passed they became accustomed to the old lady's imperious air. One day, breathing heavily, she preceded them by a pathway up the bare hillside above the villa, her silver-mounted cane raising or pushing aside strands of rusted barbed wire—a relic of World War Two. On the hilltop she showed them how to catch scorpions. 'Of course they can be cooked and eaten,' she insisted. She then showed Mary how to snap off sprigs of lavender and wild tansy.

Straightening her back she pointed with her cane at the village below, the boule-players indolently pitching, with now and again the gleam of the metal ball as it described its arc. She indicated the village and the great curve of beach that stretched from the outer rim of the row of stores and apartments and the hotel southward until it was lost in mist beside Perpignan and the border with Spain.

'The Pyrenees?' In answer to Mary's query she indicated smoke and the lick of flames in the mountains. 'The villages there are populated by lascivious dwarfs,' she said. 'Bow-legged chaps—card-players, beer-swillers and bottom-pinchers.' She cackled and crowed tolerantly. Later, when all three drove south to the mountains, Mary's lips came apart in pleasure at the cobbled streets under cool tall trees, at the mystery of dark interiors and the whispering of the ribands of coloured plastic that covered the inner doorways of the village stores.

That afternoon they passed through a village where a bull-fight was in progress. Lady Margaret, drawing the car to a halt in the shade, settled herself for a nap. She urged Mary and Joe to visit the *corrida*. They could climb to the cheaper seats in the sun and experience a rather splendid barbarity—just once!

Shading her eyes with her hand, Mary, looking down, realized that what the toreador was digging out of the shoulders of the bull was not red paint but blood. As the matador, his suit of lights stilled of twinkling, came to tiptoe to administer the *coup de grâce* her eyes narrowed. It occurred to her that at that moment, the matador, after a ritual akin to courtship, was wholly a male symbol which, by an excess of manhood, had rendered the bull female. It was as if he had willed the brute into a coupling through which manhood could be reconceived.

As the bull's forefeet buckled, the spectators around her uttered blood cries. She looked sidelong at Joe, a silly straw hat protecting his bald head. She asked herself if he had ever thought deeper than the superficial service of his sire horse. Would she herself ever become reconciled to his clumsiness? Would he ever evoke the ceremony that would lead to the abandonment of self in her or evoke the music of timelessness that was embedded in her flesh? There were mornings when she awoke trembling, to ask herself if the fingerpost that had directed her out of the house of virgins had been twisted in the night by vandals so that she had been misled into entering a territory where men, simply as nature called, gracelessly relieved their kidneys, their bowels and their loins.

Fearful of the trend of her thinking she paused: was it not her sacramental duty to obey? 'How now, brown cow?' she murmured to herself as she and Joe rejoined Lady Margaret in the car.

5

Time ticked on day after day, week after week in the villa above the village and the sea. Whenever there was desultory mention of returning to Ireland Lady Margaret frowned so that at last Mary admitted she had no firm ties of duty at home and that Joe's cousin seemed pleased at being asked to look after the stallion and the smallholding in their absence. So Mary took the rule and rhythm of the villa as once she had accepted the routine of the convent. At Lady Margaret's insistence she wore lighter clothes.

Joe busied himself about the villa and the garden. He polished the old motor-car until it gleamed in the sunlight. In the late afternoon he spent a few hours on the beach where a single revolving wave at the tide lip had scooped clifflets of sand a foot or so in height which, on collapsing, were overwhelmed by a swirl of green water. Each afternoon too, wearing his antiquated bathing costume Joe swam parallel to the shore; then, his gold tooth gleaming a greeting at those he passed, he walked along the edge of the sea towards Spain; then turning about he strolled past his starting point, moving towards the northern end of the beach and promenade where a series of rock shafts had cut off a secluded cove.

Each day during this paddle-stroll he paused to wrestle with a stubby tree trunk, the antlers of whose roots caused it grotesquely to turn on its points when taken and restored by the rolling of the wave. Each day the trunk came ashore at a different point, and, as he wrestled good-humouredly with it, Joe seemed to exude manly satisfaction at having at last found the France of his dreams.

Returned to his starting point he threw himself down between the twin hulls of a catamaran drawn up on the sand. There he seemed oblivious to the almost naked bodies of the younger women lying on their faces a short distance away. Their patronizing smiles he had come to ignore: gradually his body became an odder shade of brown-yellow.

Mary had learned to shop in the village. Each morning she took a shopping basket and, with Nikolai the borzoi on a lead, passed the boule-players and paced the narrow strip of tarmac that twisted among flimsy houses in the course of construction on her way to the stores on the seafront. As she walked along Algerian workmen stripped to the waist paused in their work to whistle through their teeth—ostensibly at the hound but, Mary guessed, more so at herself.

In the snow white *boucherie* she noted the deft way the young butcher swivelled the piece of meat on the block as he trimmed it of its fat. Carefully she watched his manner of pinching off lengths of sausages or pudding from a skein dangling overhead, the accurate way he dropped her joint of meat sidelong on the pan of the weighing machine and, finally, his method of wrapping her purchase and placing it before her. He always smiled as he handed her her change. This morning ritual made her thoughtful and a little excited. On the way home her mind retained the image of his deft hands. Some mornings she stopped to make a purchase at a stall of matted straw where a fisherman's daughter—she had once noticed her lying on the sand beside the young butcher— sold octopuses and shellfish. The girl had an ugly face but a superb body.

6

The days went by. Then Joe was drowned so simply as to border on the banal. There were only a few people on the late afternoon beach when a landwind took a boy's blue and yellow beach ball out to sea. Joe started to swim after it using his awkward breast stroke. About a hundred and fifty yards from the shore, with the ball just beyond his reach, Joe turned and began to swim back. He was well beyond his depth when his stroke weakened. He ceased to swim, his mouth opened wide; he struggled for a while before beginning to gasp for help.

The boy whose ball had drifted out to sea stood watching

stolidly as Joe choked on cries which presently dwindled into a gulping struggle for life. As the swimmer's head went down for the last time the boy looked at the ball, by then barely discernible far out to sea, and, turning, ran to join his parents.

A few late sunbathers had raised themselves on their elbows to watch Joe's final efforts. The boy's parents gathered up their clothes and moved off. They mentioned casually to the girl of the fish stall that a man had been drowned. The accident caused little stir: three men had been lost from that stretch of beach during the preceding month. The Irishman was recalled in the context of his bald head, his odd bathing costume, his brown-yellow skin and because he had given his life in an attempt to recover a ball.

After the first shock, one rather of dull disbelief than of sorrow, Mary took the matter calmly. Lady Margaret, her silver rings flashing, dealt imperiously with the gendarmerie. She showed them the dead man's passport and in the days that followed she and Mary took to pacing the promenade in the early morning hours, the pair from time to time pausing to scan the surface of the water.

Presently the morning patrol ceased; the two women drove some distance to the south to view a smelly corpse—that of a fat man, his hair jet-black, his swimming trunks bright red and the extremities of his limbs nibbled by sea-creatures.

No, it certainly was not Joe Hendron, owner of a sire horse, ex-Gaelic footballer and lover of France. The second corpse they were called upon to view some days later was undoubtedly that of Joe—the features had blackened and were further attenuated, but the hair fringe was there, falling free from the bald crown of the head, and, to place the matter beyond doubt, the pink comb peeped from its seam in the frayed costume. And if this were not enough, when the custodian of the boathouse drew back the lip of the corpse, he revealed the gold tooth gleaming in the interior of the mouth.

*   *   *

Mary, accompanying the coffin containing her husband, was met at Shannon Airport by the caretaker cousin. His greeting was anything but cordial; as they approached Teercallaghan village where they met the first of a cortège of neighbours come out to

90

pay respects, his attitude was one of surliness and hostility. A guard of honour from the local football team stopped the motor hearse and, opening the glass door, the captain ceremoniously placed a blue and gold jersey on the lid of the coffin. The cousin closed the glass door and ordered the driver to move on.

During the Requiem Mass and burial Mary remained passive. Returning to her mother's cottage after the ceremonies she found that her aunt, now retired from her nursing post, had taken up permanent residence with her sister, Mary's mother.

The day following the funeral, Mary consulted a solicitor in the nearest town. He was a heavy man with a drink-ravaged face.

'Married a little over a month, eh?' he growled. 'The farm is yours in law but country people have a different bloody law. Don't tell anyone that you intend going back to France! You'll have to sell to his cousin or have a feud on your hands. We'll make him sweat so that he'll buy in a hurry. Are you pregnant?'

'No!'

'Bloody pity in one way! If you were pregnant, you'd have a stronger claim. A blessing in another. Leaves you free. Could you manage a few pukes before breakfast and get this aunt of yours to broadcast it? Or walk out of Mass before the end with a handkerchief to your face. No? Handy way of earning a few thousand quid. A puke'd frighten the piss outa him. Keep your mind to yourself!'

Again, Mary holed up in the back room of her mother's cottage.

The aunt spread rumours of Mary's pale face. Word went round that a far-out relative of the Hendrons—a man from the Bronx—was about to buy the farm by private treaty. The caretaker cousin lost his nerve and paid dearly for the place. Mary found herself with more money than ever she had before. 'How now, brown cow?' she murmured to herself as she took her seat in the plane for France.

7

Lady Margaret, a cigarillo between her lips, met her at Perpignan. On the way home they passed the old mini-car rusting amid vines gone wild. Her Ladyship crowed: in spite of herself, Mary smiled.

She resumed her work about the house. One of the first things she did was to pitch the volcano kettle over the garden wall and into the rocky scrub and rusted wire at the back of the villa. She enjoyed the evening meal on the balcony with Lady Margaret. She bought a two-piece swim-suit and a bathing wrap in vivid colours. Most mornings she swam in the sea: in the late evenings after dinner she left the house to exercise the borzoi. The village was then quiet and the merry-go-round on the seafront completely still. From the building site came the sad Algerian music and from beyond the low sea wall the minor thunder of the single wave. The combination of dinner wine and sea air made her light-headed. Later, luxuriously, she stretched out for sleep and thought of a rook's feather caressing her naked body.

One evening of soft blue light as she walked the hound along the seafront, she saw a cigarette glow behind the wheel of a car parked on the other side of the road. She turned her head on hearing the clack of hurrying sandals and was in time to see the fisher girl enter the open door of the vehicle; the roof light showed up the face of the young butcher as he leaned over on his seat to help the girl enter. Mary walked on quickly.

Next morning in the *boucherie* his sharp glance confirmed that he knew she had witnessed the incident. She found herself blushing. A few evenings later she noticed the same car parked on the side of the seafront on which she walked. As she approached, the door opened and the young butcher got out. Lighting a cigarette and placing his back against the car, he greeted her quietly. Pretending that she did not recognize him, she moved on but he drove the car ahead of her and waited until again she had drawn level with him. He was courteous but confident. He walked beside her to the end of the promenade. Reaching the rocks that marked the limit of the beach he indicated the hidden cove below. She turned away quickly. Accompanying her as far as the car he bade her a quiet good-night—one that had a mocking smile to it.

After this she found herself waking at 3 or 4 a.m. and unable to return to sleep. She took to moving quietly on to the balcony of the villa: there, wearing only her dressing-gown, she sat looking down on the village and analysing the noises of its night. She watched the bats circling a street light semi-hidden in foliage. As a single light flicked on she recalled the old woman in the village *boulangerie*, etiolated, drained and flour-dusty, who mostly lived out her days working in the dim interior of the bakehouse.

Some evenings later (she had meanwhile temporarily changed the direction of her stroll) the young butcher joined her at the place where they had originally met. Again he kept pace with her to the end of the pavement: this time, however, as he moved down into the cove, after a pause she followed. He then lay full length beside her on the dry sand. The borzoi also stretched out listlessly and, having watched the pair for a short time, turned his attention to the swaying sea. The instant the butcher's fingers caressed her, Mary's time of restraint was as nothing. *'Ouvrez!'* he commanded. She obeyed.

They were married in the church of an inland village. The leather-padded door of the church was studded with brass nails. The pervading smell was of candlegrease and old mortar. Even in the late summer the interior of the building held elements of the previous winter's frost. The officiating curé shook as with Parkinson's disease. A civil ceremony followed. Lady Margaret queened it over both occasions. The bridegroom's name was Amedu.

After a week in Marseilles the couple went off to live in Amedu's native village in the foothills of the French Pyrenees. There he assisted his unmarried uncle who was the village butcher. The newly-married couple rented an upstairs flat in a narrow street. After heavy rain the cobbled roadway under their windows became a roaring culvert. On days of intense heat Mary looked up through the tree-tops and gravely pondered the possibility of forest fires. Now and then she could hear cries and music from the shoddy bullring of the village.

Amedu, as his fingers had already indicated, was an inventive and mercurial lover. He taught Mary ways of making love she hadn't dreamed existed. At times in the climax of coupling she apprised herself looking over her husband's bare shoulder to evoke the images of Joseph of the yellow skin and even of the Reverend Mother and Sisters of her enclosed life. At such times a remote smile touched her mouth corners and, inwardly, she asked herself the question: 'How now, brown cow?'

She gave birth to three children in successive years—two boys and a girl. Amedu shrugged his shoulders tolerantly when she insisted on naming the children Patrick, Brendan and Kathleen. Then the child-bearing stopped: she put on a little weight and her olive face grew plumper, distending her pale mole.

In moments of evasion Amedu flicked Gauloises out of pale blue packets and began a bout of chain-smoking. Then, with a laughing comrade, on the pretence of seeing the more famous bullfighters, he made trips over the mountains to Figeuras or Gerona. She knew what the pair were about but did not complain: at times she wondered dully if as a result of her husband's love forays she would contract disease. She learned to speak a modicum of vernacular French but as an element of the life about her she remained alien. She carefully concealed the fact that she had once been a nun and laid no stress on the exercise of religion. She was conscious of her life moving sluggishly forward. When the house was quiet around her she stared into the mirror for several minutes. And at such times her lips moved in the quiet query: 'How now, brown cow?'

She returned to Ireland once only—to attend the funeral of her mother. The ceremonies over, she looked around her in disbelief at the dark bogs and bare hills. Then, with a sense of relief, she hurried back to France.

8

Years later, on a Sunday afternoon in autumn, when Amedu and his companion were at the local *corrida*, Mary with her two younger children moved upwards out of the village and into the mountains. She came at last to a point in the pathway higher than ever she had reached before. Beside her was a flat sandstone rock covered with mauve butterflies; beneath the rock and around it a stream swirled, indicating by the purity of its water the presence of a parent glacier far above. The air above her was free of trees; the children were some distance away and crouched in silence on the gravelled edge of a shallow pool.

Turning her back on the peaks she looked northward to where the great plain of mid-France merged in haze with the sky. Eastward was the sea: watching it, all she could picture was a blue and yellow ball sailing regally over the waves as it lured Joe to his death. Westward, the plain below the foothills bore the sombre pillars of the cypresses. From the village below the muted sound of a brass band reached her ears.

As she continued to watch the scene, confused thoughts and superimposed images came and went in her imagination. It was as if the spread of land below her had become a wide mirror reflecting the course of her life. 'How now?' she murmured as queries came pelting in upon her. 'After all these years what have you retained of your former life? What have you sloughed? What have you gained? Are you happy or sad?—that is if happiness and sadness can be defined. On five separate occasions you have exercised a choice—have any of these choices brought you freedom? Have you not, on each occasion, chosen to re-enter a bondage of sorts? Are you not one of those who of their nature cannot tolerate personal freedom? Are the embers of your religious life still alive under the ashes of the past? If you had remained in the convent would not your mood of seeking freedom have ebbed with the passing of time? Now that women are adding a novel dimension to the religious life would you not have found fulfilment? Would not the recurrent image of the rook's feather have then become a symbol transcending that of sensuous dalliance? How now, brown cow?'

In a flickering succession of images she pictured the polished parquetry of the convent and the red glow of its sanctuary lamp. There followed the distended nostrils of Marengo as a neigh issued from between his stripped teeth; then it was the smoke belch from the volcano kettle, Joe's features as he viewed the Mona Lisa, the feeling of drenched cloth clinging to her breasts, Lady Margaret's cockcrow, scorpions under grey stones, her palms raised so that she could smell crushed tansy, the clinking of silver balls, the gold tooth in the boathouse, the jersey on the coffin, the blood-crowded features of the solicitor. Algerian music too and the fisher girl lying on hot sand and finally the deft hands of Amedu. Sensation and recollection, wistful and rebellious, chaste and errant, crowded round her shouting like a mob until she clapped her hands over her ears and squeezed her eyes shut as does a child. 'How now?' the mob continued to howl. Then the noise ceased abruptly.

She was remotely conscious of a great silence pervading the world. She opened her eyes and slowly removed her hands from her ears. The stream beside her seemed to have ceased its hollow hubbub and the butterflies covering the rockface were overlords of a noiseless realm. From the bullring on the edge of the village below a spurt of applause was followed by a return to intense silence. She now knew what the silence signified—at this moment the matador, his suit of lights stilled of its twinkling, had raised himself to tiptoe and was aiming his swordpoint so as to finish off the bull. Wait! she counselled herself. Then she heard the crowd release its hoarded frenzy in a roar of triumph and appreciation. The bull would now have taken the blade fully: already its legs were buckling beneath it.

Mary closed her eyes and, one with the penetrated animal, staggered and almost fell. For she too, in the penitence of a nun and the ecstasy of a lover, was welcoming the blade fully into her own body. As again the roar came up, this time with blood on it, she faked dying in mimicry of the brute below.

After a few moments she shook her head clear of imagery. She identified her surroundings, called briskly to her children and began to walk downward to the village.

Confessions at Carhoo

As if pondering deeply, his jaw sunken on his lugs, his blue eyes watching through the parting in the faded red curtains before him, the parish priest of Carhoo was seated in the confession box of his church.

The afternoon sunlight striking down through the stained glass of a window cast a sprawl of red, blue, yellow and purple on the mellow pews. Except for the ticking of a clock the church was soundless. Except for the presence of the priest the church appeared to be empty.

The old man drew a red handkerchief from his sleeve and began to pat his forehead. Replacing the handkerchief he rested his forearm on the wooden projection by his left arm. Though his gaze was steady on the patch of colour outside something in his pose suggested that his mind was circling, roving from a central point out and around.

For a time the priest breathed deeply but quietly. His quiet breathing indicated that there would be few penitents today. A sound like a grunt escaped him as he glanced sidelong and down at his tattered breviary. There was no hurry, he told himself: he had long since recited the matins and lauds of the day's office. Vespers and compline could be read in the open air later in the afternoon.

From over the whitethorn hedges outside, their leaves touched with the first of autumn, drifted the sound of a phrase of music being played over and over on a trombone. That would be the circus, he told himself; here today, gone tomorrow. Beyond the phrase of music he could catch other faint sounds in the meadows below the bogland: mostly the faraway cries of children.

The priest locked his hands under his loose stomach. His eyes closing almost imperceptibly he began to sink into himself, even to tilt sideways a little. Although his body was in repose, it vaguely conveyed the sense of being alert. And still more vaguely there was the sense of the circling mind.

From behind a pillar in the church came the voice of an old woman raised in prayer. The priest growled in his throat; his eyes barely opened, then closed. That would be Annie the Moon, pestering the Almighty with requests for the safe delivery of her niece's infant or for the speedy return of her nephew, a private soldier in the peace-keeping force in the Lebanon. Again the old man's head swayed, then sank awkwardly on his breast. Tentatively he began to snore.

The afternoon ticked on.

As the sound of snoring grew louder, Annie the Moon uncoiled in her faded black shawl. Bent with age, her lips gabbling soundlessly, she emerged from behind the pillar. As she waddled across the church by the Communion rail, her eyes kept darting here and there. Swivelling to face the tabernacle, she bowed her head still lower in lieu of genuflection.

Reaching the confessional, with her left hand she clutched her shawl underneath her chin, so that her ashen wrinkled face was framed by the dark material. The snores continuing, she drew aside one of the curtains and peeped into the box. Light fell upon the face of the sleeping priest. Watching him, the old woman's face became curiously affectionate. She let the curtain fall slowly and, still gabbling without sound, returned to her place behind the pillar.

Motes whirled slowly in the strong shaft of sunlight. In the red bowl of colza oil in the tabernacle lamp the wick burned without quirk. On an old mosaic on the sanctuary wall the cloak of a resurrection-blinded soldier glowed in mossy green. There was a lingering odour of candlewax and incense. Here and there brass was bright. Merging into the silence of the church the clock ticked on.

*　　*　　*

The head of a clown appeared above the wall surrounding the yard outside. The face was white and blotched with large red spots; the exaggerated mouth was locked in a huge grin. From under a conical cap tufts of red wig protruded.

The clown climbed on to the wall; he sat on it for a moment

then eased his elongated boots down to the grassy hummock of a grave. Securely on the ground, he snatched off his cap and stumbled towards the side door of the church. In the porch he dipped his fingertips in the holy water stoup, crossed himself without touching his forehead and entered the building.

For a moment or two he stood inside the inner doorway. Craning his neck he looked at the confession box. As he did so he clutched his cap against his pierrot suit over which he wore a loose overcoat patterned in huge check. A faint flicker entered his eyes as he heard the snoring of the priest. He bobbed his knee in the direction of the sanctuary, then knelt in a pew not far from the door. As he prayed, his eyes took in the building. Presently he bent his head, and his spread fingers dug tensely into his wig. His knuckles stood out whitely against the absurd-coloured hair.

From the confessional came an extra loud snore.

The clown rose, tiptoed forward, opened the penitents' compartment nearest him, entered, closed the door behind him and knelt beneath the rectangle of mesh. A black crucifix with a silver Christ hung above him. Through the carved opening at the top of the door a dim light entered in quatrefoil pattern.

The sound of the priest's snoring was augmented by the wood of the confessional.

After a time the clown began to tap with his fingernail on the mesh. The snoring ceased momentarily and was then resumed in an altered key. As, again, a further series of taps brought the same result, the clown rose and came out into the church. He moved forward and peered in at the sleeping priest. As he was about to tap on the side of the door Annie the Moon's voice pealed out in supplication:

'Divine Lord, save me from arthritis and diseases of women. All-powerful God, hear the prayer of an old woman who will soon meet you face to face.'

The clown looked over his shoulder. He could see no one. Again he slipped into the penitents' compartment and drew the door to behind him. Going on his knees he coughed loudly and noised his long boots.

There was a pause. Then, almost without sound, the slide behind the mesh was drawn.

The clown hastily crossed himself. All he could see at first was the great ear of the priest framed in the fork of a thumb and four fingers. Then, vaguely beyond the perforated screen, he made out the strong nose and the blue eye.

'My child?'

'Bless me, Vater, I have sin. It's much time since my last confession.'

The priest's head stiffened. His nose twitched. The blue eyes swivelled and looked fully into the clown's face.

'Who are you? What's the meaning of this?'

'I am a clown from der Zirkus. I have not told my sins for many years.'

'Why have you come here dressed up like this?'

'The grace of God come on me quick. If I wait, it will be gone.'

A pause. The priest relaxed. His ear came closer to the white and red face. Quietly, 'How long is it since your last confession?'

'Fifteen year—twenty, twenty-five. I do not know.'

'Tell me your sins.'

The grotesque mouth came closer to the mesh. The great lips curled about the words.

'Sins of the flesh, Vater, some of nature others not of nature. In many towns of Europe. Night after night, year after year—many sins.'

'Go on!'

'There were prostitutes. I must have put virgins with child—with the next day, I go. Their names, their faces—all are gone.

'Francs, roubles, pesetas, piastres, pounds, I have stolen. I have been in prison or I would not be with a miserable Zirkus in a little country. I have been drunk so many times that at last I am verrückt—yes, I am mad. I have brushed vermin from my sleeves where there were no vermin at all.'

'Go on.'

'What city it was in France I do not know. It was by the sea—perhaps St Malo or La Rochelle. I strike a man on the head with an iron spike and I smash his skull. My friends and I, we tell the gendarmes that he fall from a wagon. But it was not so, *mein Vater* —I kill him like you kill a swine.'

The confession went on.

The priest's mind was circling. It seemed to him that his ear was in the centre of a great wheel. On the outer felloes were red jewels—these were rapes, murders and blasphemies. The diamonds encrusting the spokes were cafés and bistros, brothels and bordellos of night-lit cities in Europe. The noise the wheel made as it turned was that of a roulette wheel. There was also the flash of playing cards and the rattle of shaken dice. Smoke was in the air. Women's breasts were almost bare.

The penitent paused in his recital. He bowed his mock-bald head. Then the grotesque hair came slowly up.

'In *der Zirkus* now there is a young equestrienne—her husband trains the puppies, Bon and Paris, Chérie and Garçon.'

'Do not identify anyone!'

'This girl is inside my head all of the day, all of the night. *Ach!* When we pitch the tent on grass, as now, the grass speaks with passion. Her eyes tell me *"Ja, ja!"* Here is a temptation greater than I am.'

'Is that all?'

'That is all.'

From the fields about the church came the cries of children. A new phrase of music was being played on the trombone. There was a muted neighing of horses and a distant shrill yapping of dogs.

The priest spoke sidelong. 'As for your past sins I see your coming to confession as an indication of your sorrow. When you killed this man, since it is difficult to isolate motives, it may have been manslaughter, still one of the most serious of crimes. In your present temptation avoid nearness and tenderness. You have led a very dissolute life and anything that I say may be inadequate. However, though God hates the sin He loves the sinner. There is joy in heaven at your repentance. For these and all the sins of your past life, are you now most truly sorry?'

'I am.'

'For your penance say one Pater and five Aves in honour of the Immaculate Conception. Make an Act of Sorrow.'

The clown recited the Act of Contrition in German. Now and again he paused as if to search for forgotten words. The light from the church was lost and found on the priest's hand as he made the sign of the Cross.

'God bless you!' the confessor said, his hand moving to the slide.

'*Vater,*' the clown said hoarsely. From his breast he took out an oblong of faded pasteboard. 'A ticket for *der Zirkus*,' he said inserting it in a break in the mesh.

The priest allowed himself a wintry smile. Then he nodded, took the piece of pasteboard and drew the slide.

The clown, his head in his hands, knelt for a few moments in a pew close to the doorway. He looked up from the recital of his penance and stared into the sallow face of Annie the Moon. Watching him the old woman's jaw had dropped in amazement. The clown pulled a still more grotesque face so that she started away. Snatching his cap from under his arm he came to his feet. At the doorway he turned, spread his arms, stiffened his body and pulled an outlandish grin at her. He then left the church, swivelled over the wall and clumped across the field in the direction of the tent.

In the confessional the priest sat erect, his blue eyes fixed on the pews. The ticking of the clock became audible to him again. Just as his hand had gone into his sleeve to take out his handkerchief he heard Annie the Moon approaching. He heard her stumbling into the side of the confessional opposite to that previously occupied by the clown. When the old woman had blundered to her knees the priest drew the slide and inclined his great ear towards the mesh.

'Yes?' he said sternly.

'There was a painted man in the church, Father!'

'How long is it since your last confession?'

'A week, Father.'

'Tell me your sins!'

The old woman gulped, then recovered. 'Twice I watered milk and sold it as full milk. I found a half flitch o' bacon and never looked for the owner. I bought a rail of turf I knew was stolen. When my daughter's cow slung her calf I threw the sling into a neighbour's field so that abortion would melt his herd. I planted eggs in a farmer's garden to bring him bad luck. I stole two Apostle spoons at a wake in Monaster. I have a habit of saying "God blast you" to the ass . . .'

'Go on,' the priest said wearily.

'I took a woman's character away by saying that she'd steal the eye out of your head. I was late for Mass one Sunday—the veil was off the chalice and I never went to another. When I was up before the court for having no licence for my dog, I kissed my thumb instead of the book and said something that could be either this or that. There was a boy handled me in a hayshed some years back and, God forgive me, I remembered it and enjoyed the memory.'

'Have you already confessed these sins?'

'Some of them, Father.'

'No need to go over them again. Anything else?'

The old woman's recital went on. Again the illusion of the turning wheel took the priest's mind. Iron rim, felloes, spokes, hub and greased axle all had fused to become a cartwheel daubed with mud and dung. What he could dimly discern in the slow spinning he construed as wake-rooms with eyes glittering under shawls, yeast-smelling public houses, the smoked rafters of the last of the thatched cabins, tongues and fangs busy with evil, the glitter of black bogwater under a scurrying moon, the hiss of potatoes being sliced into seed, lime piercing the split fingers of old women, and superstition writhing in its final death-throes. The stone figure of a fertility image, her thighs spread, her breasts disproportionately large, leered at him from her point of poise above the revolutions of the wheel.

The image of the wheel faded as the circus band began to play. The music suggested piebald ponies rearing in *haute école*, the supple body of an equestrienne somersaulting on a horse's back. It evoked the picture of the clown falling over his boots and the dog trainer dressed in top hat and cutaway coat with poodles standing on their hind legs, their front paws begging for favours.

Sharply the priest recalled his wandering thoughts. 'Contagious abortion in cattle is the curse of the countryside! Taking the name of God in vain is a grave sin against the Second Commandment. A person's character is his or her most precious possession. The Lord said, "Remember that thou keep holy the Sabbath day." Calling down God to witness a lie in court is perjury—a sin until recently reserved for forgiveness by the bishop alone. Going over bad thoughts and taking pleasure in them is a folly that mocks grey hairs.'

The woman groaned.

'For your penance say a Rosary and do the Stations of the Cross. Now make an Act of Sorrow.'

'O my God, I am heartily sorry . . .'

After Annie the Moon had left the box and gone mumbling to her place behind the pillar the priest continued to sit erect. Then he softly drew the slide on the side in which the clown had made his confession. Putting his nose close to the mesh he drew the smell of circus through one of his nostrils. His eyes unwinking, he closed the slide and after a time he drew it on the side on which Annie the Moon had confessed. As he placed his other nostril close to the mesh the smell of burned faggots and old shawl came out to him. He closed the slide and for a time he sat without movement.

When he had ensured that the old woman had left the building the priest took up his breviary and after a moment's hesitation inserted the circus ticket among its pages. He then left his compartment, glanced about the empty church, genuflected to the tabernacle and donned his biretta. As he walked towards the side door he drew the violet stole from around his neck, kissed the cross embroidered on it and began to fold it. Outside, where he looked younger than when seated in the confessional, he locked his breviary in his armpit and began to pace up and down on the flagged pathway that edged the northern wall of the nave. As he paced he set his broad shoulders well back and clasped his hands behind his back. His face paled in the autumn air and slender veins stood out like threads on his cheekbones.

Soon a burst of mingled applause and laughter from the circus tent made him pause. With a quick glance about him he turned off the pathway and, walking in the hollow between two rows of grass-overgrown graves, came to a halt beside the wall. Leaning his forearms on the top of it he looked over the brilliant grass, over the whitethorn bushes, towards the faded green and white stripes of the tent with its tattered pennants barely wagging in the slight breeze. With the shrill barking of dogs came commingled laughter and applause: it was a torrent of noise in the quiet air.

After a time the priest drew the pasteboard ticket from his breviary and read the legend on it. Slowly he tore the ticket across again and again until he had made small pieces of it. These he cupped in his left hand and poured into a triangular flaw in the masonry on the top of the uncapped wall.

As he turned to move away he found a piece of the pasteboard adhering to the front of his soutane. He picked it off, rested it on his palm, then brought his pursed lips close to it and blew.

The scrap fluttered over and over in the air; then, falling freely to the ground, it was lost from his sight among the rank grasses of a grave.

The French Cradle

I

The period of my Fulbright scholarship having ended and my library research being more or less completed, I prepared to leave Oxford at the beginning of summer. I did so with mixed feelings, for now I was about to undertake the field work necessary for the completion of my dissertation. But, as yet, I had no intimation of the turmoil that was in store for me.

As an American woman in Europe for the first time, I had grown to regard with affection and respect, not only Somerville College where I had spent the previous year, but also very many aspects and landmarks of the old city. The pale gold tower of Magdalen, the willows trailing in Isis water, the fuss of the morning market, the hush of libraries and bookshops (Blackwell's unfolding, room after booklined room, like a series of Chinese boxes) and the aloof Tory air of the Randolph Hotel—these had become part of me. I liked especially the atmosphere of the old inns, not merely those such as the Mistress Quickly in an entry off Cornmarket in mid-city but those in the surrounding countryside—The Trout close to Godstow Bridge with a ruined nunnery in the fields across the Thames, The Lamb in Burford and those in mellow villages like the Slaughters—Upper and Lower—set deep in the Cotswolds.

Some of those inns, before which I liked to sit and sip mild ale, had names vaguely reminiscent of my European errand. The Nag's Head, The Swan's Head and The Admiral's Head—these were recurrent reminders of the nature of the field-work that lay before me. Thoughtful in young summer, I looked back on my humid yet vivid Georgian farming background (peaches, pecans and corn), superimposing upon it the cool appointments of my Oxford experience. I now found myself enriched as a scholar but—this I barely articulated—unfulfilled as a woman. For I had come to realize that for me the tide of fertile life was ebbing. By American standards I was no longer young. Whenever I looked into a mirror the word 'bluestocking' came readily to my lips.

So even as I looked forward with apprehension to the travel and research, most of it in the open air of Celtic Europe, part of me welcomed the harshness of effort it would entail, remotely hoping that it would prove more than mere research. And even as I barely formulated this hope, the inn sign of The Saracen's Head above me creaked and grated in an unexpected breeze.

Let me now introduce myself:

Name: Louanne Brigid Dobbs. *Occupation*: Lecturer in Ethnohistory. *Age and Marital Status*: Thirty, unmarried. *Place of Birth*: Montezuma, Georgia, USA. *Place of Residence*: ditto. *Appearance*: Ordinary. *Temperament*: Superficially placid. *Future*: Appears set for a university teaching career as indicated by acceptance of doctoral dissertation. *Title of Dissertation*: 'The Cult of the Severed Head in Celtic Mythology'. *Thesis Adviser*: Dr Robert Thorpe, Dept. of Ethnohistory, University of Georgia, Athens. *Reason for Acceptance of Thesis*: (Remote) Incautious mention of maternal great-great-grandmother Brigid O'Leary. (Proximate) Impending vacancy in relevant department of University of Ga.

Professor Thorpe, pale grey suit, white shirt, white tie, white hair, bland round face smiling like a white cat at my recital of the reception my defence of the subject had received from the Ph. D. Committee. He had foisted the subject on me: the name Brigid had given him the excuse. 'Your research may prove rewarding,' he purred, adding slowly, 'On many levels.' I was not convinced that my choice of subject was the correct one. For even at that early stage I knew that, as a woman, I should have been more interested in the creation of life than in the ritualistic celebration of its destruction.

2

I roamed at will, mostly through Middle Europe. I crossed frontiers as on a slender clue or whim, at times retracing my steps to verify a belated conclusion. In the light of a blood-red sunset I squinted at Celto-Ligurian statuary on a site close to the mouth of the Rhone. At Roquepertuse in the same area, standing in a

Celtic sanctuary, I gaped at a huge stone bird presiding over pillar holes that had once contained human heads. At Entremont, to the east, there was a hillock of human skulls. Crossing from France into Italy to seek out traces of the Gallo-Celts I examined the Manerbio necklace, an ornament composed of a series of heads ranged about a swastika.

Moving northwards again through France, the Gallo-Roman sanctuary of Sequena near the source of the Seine rewarded me with a gentler series of heads carved from wood. Pfalsfeld on the Rhine had a treasure house of artefacts recovered from Celtic mounds in the area. La Tène in Switzerland and Hallstatt of the Austrian salt mines are places that have given their names to significant phases of Celtic art: these in turn I visited, finding with rather grim satisfaction examples of carved severed heads grotesque in the extreme.

Still on the Continent I paid a visit to Silkenborg Museum in Denmark there to examine the preserved head of the Tollund Man, which for me had a ritualistic significance inasmuch as it represented a human sacrifice to a Celtic Goddess. Indeed, wandering in this heartland of world culture, and recalling that the Celts had established the first civilization north of the Alps I realized that I was rummaging among the debris of the 4th-century BC Celtic kingdoms of central and western Europe where once a female deity akin to Aphrodite and Ishtar, often depicted as naked and uplifting her breasts in a milk-giving gesture, was greatly revered—and feared.

I was vaguely tempted to visit Galatia in what was once Asia Minor, and even Iceland which has a Celtic seam to its folktales, but successfully resisted the temptations. However, I readily succumbed to the calls of Brittany, Cornwall, Wales and the Isle of Man and also spent a week amid howling winds on the Outer Hebrides, my pencil busy and my tiny camera clicking all the while. Returned to Oxford and to the summer crowds milling around Carfax, I paused before my final journey westward to take stock of my progress, academic and indeed, as I later discovered, highly personal.

3

I had already reached firm—some of them rather obvious—conclusions.

First, the cult of the severed head was not confined to the Celtic peoples: my prime problem was to isolate relevant facts in a vast spread of research, this because tribes of different racial origins, by ritualized familiarity with this grisly fetish, had hoped thereby to overcome their innate terror of the world of shade. For me, each new revelation of the cult had shown nuances, arabesques, feints, convolutions, laminations and, as it were, palimpsests of approach indicating a wide range of attitude ranging from terror to affection. Again, in some of the rituals, the themes of mating birth and death were interwoven so as to remind one of the interlacing in early illuminated manuscripts. The presence of birds, beasts, fishes and above all reptiles encircling human heads in the ornamentation of these manuscripts—mostly of monastic origin—seemed to point to the conflict between paganism and Christianity.

The skull too, I found, filled a variety of roles. I noted it as a children's toy, as a drinking vessel, as a seal or symbol impressed on wedding confectionery. It also appeared as an architectural enrichment, as a mnemonic or reminder of man's end, as a friend or closer than friend, as an item of battle booty which, when embalmed in cedar oil, was proudly displayed to guests. These roles were comparable to boundary marks on the frontiers of the twilit territory I sought to enter.

Hitherto, my travelling and the active life it entailed had caused me to look outside of myself. But with the first cessation of effort, I found myself moving inwards upon my attitudes and emotions. Still keeping an outward eye on the aim of my dissertation, on a deeper and more intimate level I felt with conviction that if I chanced upon the core of the cult, say by stumbling on a ritual, anecdote, legend or tale that would reverberate in my blood, forces within me would be released that would resolve the tensions of my scholarly spinsterhood. So even while I resumed my interim checking and rechecking in the Bodleian, I kept reverting to this —an as yet vague conviction. Or rather, it kept reverting to me.

In what seemed a natural consequence of this conviction I now possessed (in my imagination) the head of a typical Celt of two and a half millennia before—that of a man in his prime.

In rough outline and almost in abstract design it formed an equilateral triangle standing on a blunted apex. The eye-rims were protuberant about empty sockets; the nose, a smaller triangle, sat squarely on its base in midface, its shape proportionate to the face as a whole. The mouth was a strong slit hidden beneath a moustache which drooped over the mouth corners and which, together with the bushy eyebrows, appeared as if sculpted on a head of bronze.

It was difficult to superimpose features or eye-pupils on this abstract concept, but, in the fleeting moments when I tried to do so I imagined the complexion as fair to russet and the eyes as sea-blue. Trunk and limbs eluded me, nor did they seem necessary to complete the concept, for it was this abstract head alone, for the Celts the seat of all the emotions, focused and blurred by turn, that had accompanied me in my travels and remained with me in Oxford. It was as if I were a witch (or fallen goddess!) and the head my familiar.

During this pause in my work, I also found myself subject to a disturbing psychic compression. This inner tension revealed itself in minor memory lesions, tremors, reveries, broken sleep patterns, moments of absolute fear when after waking I found myself wholly conscious but unable to move a limb, and subject to whims and tantrums such as assail a ripe or pregnant woman. Georgia with its orange-red clay, its awnings of spanish moss over drowsy rivers, its blinding sunshine, now seemed aeons removed from the dim world I had chosen to enter.

It was in this frame of mind that I crossed to Ireland.

4

Ireland seemed populated by severed heads. In the Library of Trinity College, Dublin, I found grotesque faces peering at me from the intricate ornamentation of the Book of Kells; a particularly memorable head was tucked away at the terminal of the capital P on the negram page of that astonishing volume. In museums, I came upon heads on tankards, on horned helmets, on shield bosses, on reliquaries, on grave slabs, on belt buckles recovered from sunken ships, on torc terminals, on scabbards and even on an antique but once workaday utensil known as the Marlborough bucket. I also noted miniature heads carved from amethyst staring at me from the convolutions of the Tara brooch.

On the islands of Lough Erne, I found noble heads cut from stone. One was Janus-faced. (There too I was both intrigued and revolted at finding among the heads the figure of a female in the lewdest possible posture—a representation of a forgotten goddess of fertility in middle Europe whose cult still exists in Ireland in the depraved form of reverence for Síle na gCíoch or Sheila of the Paps.) A short distance away stood a three-faced, one-headed stone representation of God the All-seeing. Later still, I delighted in the craftsmanship of the doorway of Clonfert Cathedral on the banks of Shannon River in the very centre of Ireland, its dominant glory a half-circle of stone heads.

Heads and again heads I found as finials on doorways, on gable copings, on window mouldings. Wood is a perishable material, yet further heads were mine as I traced their outlines as caryatids at the bases of eroded pillars or in the recesses of ambones. Heads were yet again depicted in the mouths of monsters on dredged-up pottery shards. Several of the superb high crosses found adjacent to old monastic sites yielded me heads. (Where on earth was it that I saw, whether in vellum, metal, wood or stone, a representation of rats gnawing a Sacred Host while a crouched cat looked on stoically? So intent was I on seeking heads that the import of the representation passed me by at the time, to return in outline at a later date.)

I laboured long in the Irish libraries. I could not even attempt to indicate the many references to the Celts from Strabo onwards in which warriors were described as riding home from battle with the freshly severed heads of their enemies tied to their belts by the flowing hair.

5

In the Department of Folklore I found many folktales relevant to the subject of my dissertation. Two in particular held me in love

and horror: the story of Bó Bóinne and the Singing Heads and
that of Dermot of the Foreigners—he who brought the Normans
to Ireland in 1169. In this latter tale Dermot is described as
rummaging among the struck-off heads of his enemies, until,
finding the head of him who had blinded his son, he picked it up,
chewed off the nose and lips and spat the pulp on the ground.
This grim incident had precedents in the classical tale of Tydeus
chewing the severed head of Mehanlippus through to the brains
and being punished by Athene who denied him the healing herb
that would have saved his life.

So as to draw still closer to such legends, I undertook a Com-
pressed Course for Beginners in the Irish language. A team of
young fanatical teachers chanting, drumming and repeating for
twelve hours a day every week-day for three weeks, drilled the
elements of the language into my head, which by this time seemed
severed from my body. For me, it was an exhausting experience.
But it worked!

Dazed as I was when, at the end of the course, I staggered out
into the sunlight, I was pleased with my newfound ability to grasp
the drift of tales in the original Irish. I also felt confident too that
I could carry on a simple conversation with a native speaker of
the western seaboard.

*   *   *

As summer advanced, I realized that it was unwise to proceed
further in this direction. I had already reached a point where I
could scarcely pass a man on Grafton Street without imagining his
sliced-off head dangling from my belt. Now truly, I was the
biblical Judith incarnate.

Throwing together the harvest of material that had accrued to
me—guide books, photographic material, tapes, photostat copies
of newspaper and magazine articles, brochures, postcards, reference books, a bulging ring-bound notebook, several smaller note-
books, my slides, my portable typewriter with several reams of
good paper, the more precious material strapped in an old army
canvas bag and slung across my shoulder, I headed south-west to
the Irish-speaking tip of the Dingle peninsula, the most westerly
part not merely of Ireland but of Europe. There, near the village
of Ballyferriter, I rented a south-facing cottage which had as its

northern backdrop the upward swoop of volcanic cliffs known as The Three Sisters. Whenever I climbed to the clifftop I fancied I could skim a stone into the Blasket Islands, while in the distant south the flanks of the Skelligs Rocks glistened like shattered mirrors.

Before proceeding to assemble my material in orderly form, I decided to let myself go slack for some time. Late summer found me loitering on a nearby beach under a high cliff, or at evening visiting one or other of the village pubs. Presently I was living quietly on the perimeter of what I call vernacular existence yet keenly observing what was going on around me. Always a good mimic, I was able to strike the exact pitch and tone of everyday greetings in Irish, so that in the mixed company of fishermen, small farmers and Irish-speaking visitors I was tolerably able to pass muster.

I dissembled in another way. Long since, the Georgian descendants of Brigid O'Leary had sloughed off whatever traces of Catholicism they once had and had become church-going Baptists. Yet, with the aim of seeing and hearing from the inside, I began to attend Sunday Mass in the copper-roofed village church, invariably seeking out an inconspicuous pew in the aisle where, as often as not, I sat between or beside two old women—the last in the parish to wear shawls.

Little by little I was taken for granted by the neighbours: every year the locality has one or two romantics like me who long to return to the simple life. I was referred to as *Í Siúd*—Her Beyond —or less often as Breed, the Irish for Brigid pronounced phonetically. The summer was the finest, the locals told me, for fifty years: by my home standards it was moderately cool even on its warmest day.

The cottage I rented was hemmed around with wild fuchsia bushes; the scarlet and purple pendants of their flowers were perfect foils for the dark green of the leaves and the pale saffron rods of the shrub itself. Whenever it rained, the stark colours of the bushes were renewed. There, during that summer-end, I worked lazily, slept late, ate well, sunbathed or dived into breakers which sometimes flung me against the tan floor of the beach, almost beheading me as they did so.

*   *   *

With the arrival of the first days of fall, I found my inner quest for a missing element increasing in intensity. At times I discovered myself hunting for it on the borderline between the subconscious and the conscious. I also was aware that I hunted as a woman, dwelling utterly within the confines of her own body.

During this period I recorded sporadically. The legend of Walter Ralegh, Fort del Oro and the Field of the Heads I set down faithfully but, odd as it sounds, for me these tales were peripheral inasmuch as they had to do with a *multitude*. For by now I sought only one.

Yet, in the physical sense, for me that summer was a time first of recuperation, then of renewal, and finally of anticipation. Whatever of value would reach me would find in me a willing ally. Day after day I watched the few bare sycamore trees in that countryside to see if their leaves were turning brittle, thus signalling that it was time for me to leave.

Meanwhile there was late sunlight to be appreciated, mushrooms to be collected, the legendary bed of the lovers Diarmuid and Gráinne to be sought for in high bracken, mackerel and pollock to be jigged for from the stern of a canvas currach, beaches to be trodden barefooted, prickly mountains to be climbed, idiotic novelettes to be read, grace-noted songs to be listened to and, above all, the sea in its moods of fury and tranquillity, its hours of noon and midnight, to be watched and evaluated.

6

A quality which the socio-anthropologist must possess is the ability to listen with interest, no matter how superficially unprepossessing the source, so as to appreciate what is being said and to be prudent enough not to show this appreciation overtly. In the case of peasant informants, recording by cassette can on occasion be a totally inhibiting factor as can overt note-taking. So the field worker is generally forced to rely on his or her own memory. (Memorandum to Field Workers in the Preparation of Dissertations)

*   *   *

The man who entered the pub was wild-eyed. Under his tattered jacket his chest was a mat of close white curls. His homespun grey trousers were patched at the knees and kept up by a piece of rope tied about his waist. His boots were slashed as if to let sea-water in and out. His wind-chapped face was littered with spikes of white beard. From under the twisted peak of his frayed cap, his dark eyes watched me. He stood there, an old jute sack slung over his shoulder. He could have been the Churl of the Drab Coat—a character out of Irish legend—come to life.

From the kitchen of the pub came a clatter of tea things. It was darkish in the bar and a little too early for evening customers. When the publican came out to serve the newcomer I called for a glass of beer which I did not need. First turning his face to the wall and glancing suspiciously over his shoulder at me, the wild-eyed man took coins from an inside pocket of his jacket. Having served the drinks in silence the publican, with a meaning-ful glance in my direction, returned to the kitchen. The tattered fellow and myself were alone in the waning daylight. Between sips of stout he glanced at me.

When I addressed him in Irish—not directly, for I looked down at the floor as I spoke—he glared sidelong without replying. For the next three-quarters of an hour I stalked him; then, knocking gently on the bar-top with the bottom of my glass to call for yet another drink which again I did not need, I also ordered a pint of stout which I signalled to the publican to place before the other customer. The publican's eyes kept warning me to be careful. Later, as my fellow customer growled a guttural remark, half in Irish, half in English, indicating that he had been secretly observ-ing my activities, I recognized that I was face to face with some-thing of importance.

The story he told me in Irish and in broken English took three weeks of erratic encounters before I drained all I could from the narrator. The tale had to do with events that happened in the area in the year 1691 and had been passed from father to son down the centuries. The tale had survived revolt, famine, eviction, emigration, degradation and some degree of modernization. It had to do with the severed head of a young man called Manning, the first of that surname in the peninsula. It also had to do with a coffer or small chest which in my own mind I named the French Cradle.

I followed that tale as a love-crazy woman pursues the object of her desire. Evening after evening, at the slackest hour in the bar, I plied the wild fellow with drink and questions until the first customers of the night began to enter. When the lights were turned on, he left abruptly. I found out where he lived—in one of the last thatched cabins of the area, a one-roomed smoky hole with only a glimmer of turf fire glinting on the stripped pole that held the sagging roof in place. On the excuse that I had lost my way I entered. It was certainly rat- and flea-infested: occasionally I saw small bright eyes reflecting firelight from a dark corner and also, after leaving the place at midnight, there were times when I had to strip to my skin and shake my clothes in a bushy corner of a field.

After a few visits, during which he doled out parts of the tale, I had the impression that my narrator was glad to be rid of the burden of the story. It was as if it were a custodial duty imposed on him by former generations. 'Mebbe I'm the last one to have it,' was a phrase he reverted to often. Eventually he began to growl me away, but I still kept quietly dunning him until I realized that there was no more to be had. Returning to my cottage after each visit I scribbled down the details while they were still fresh in my mind. At last I was satisfied that I had a fairly complete version of the centuries-old tale.

7

Standing inside the small window of her cabin in Ballyoughteragh, Seán Manning's wife, Sibil, watched the two figures move upwards from the rutted roadway below.

She had earlier seen them disembark from the white boat now drawn up on the beach. As they drew nearer she saw clearly that one was a foreign officer and the other a sailor. Must be the Frenchies, she told herself, for on his dawn return from fishing Seán had said that ships of the French fleet stood out from the mouth of Dingle harbour. He had counted eighteen ships of the line and twenty-four smaller vessels. Tales of the trouble in wider Ireland had already filtered into the peninsula. With Limerick under siege, Sibil Manning knew that soldiers of any kind meant trouble. She also knew that with Dingle and its English garrison only eight miles away news of foreign soldiers having landed would quickly reach that town.

The woman glanced anxiously towards the *cailleach* or enclosed part of the kitchen where her husband lay sprawled asleep. With chill intuition she connected the coming of the strangers with the fact that Seán was from Limerick.

From the darkness inside the half-doors of neighbouring cabins people were watching. Then the gaudy officer stood in the sunlight outside the door of the Manning cabin. He began to address the woman in courteous French, which the *matelot* beside him translated into indifferent English. Manning's wife also had indifferent English: she gathered that the strangers wished to speak to her husband, Seán Manning.

Her man was tired, she pleaded. Placing her joined hands to her temple and inclining her head, she mimed sleep. He had been fishing all night and had returned at dawn. His work was hard when the harvest mackerel filled the sea. The pair persisted, the officer firmly but courteously crossing the threshold, so that at last the woman shook her husband awake. The officer's eyes tightened on seeing the powerful head of Manning, his fingers digging into the deep-set eye-sockets as he forced himself awake. With sidelong glances the newcomers conveyed that they wished the woman to move out of doors before they made their business known.

'*C'est vous, Jean Manning?*'

They seemed to know all about Manning. They understood that he had once served in the Irish Army; also that in search of adventure he had rowed his black canoe from under the Abbey walls in Limerick, down the ebbing Shannon and out into the Atlantic, swinging in a wide arc that brought him ashore in Smerwick harbour at the top of the peninsula. There he had resumed his trade of fisherman. There too he had married and hoped to end his days in peace. All this was conveyed—the officer speaking in French, the *matelot* translating.

But things were different now, the officer went on. French men-of-war under Admiral Renaud stood off-shore. They had come to the aid of Limerick—of Ireland. Limerick under Sarsfield would soon fall if not relieved. Navigation on the Shannon was difficult. '*L'Amiral Renaud voudroit un pilote pour nos vaisseaux remonter l'estuaire jusqu'à Limerick.*'

Manning dragged on his homespun trousers, his knitted gansey and his rawhide pampooties. He walked to the doorway. The bulk of Mount Brandon filled the eastern sky. The officer waited for a reply.

There was a flurry of hens from the adjoining *cróitín*; Sibil Manning entered the kitchen carrying some freshly laid eggs. '*Cad tá uatha?*' she asked him in a low voice. Manning, his carven face filled with the light of northern sky, answered in Gaelic in a voice equally low, 'To pilot the ships to Limerick.' 'You'll get your death out of that,' the wife said sharply. Manning reflected for a moment or two, then turned to face the waiting pair. 'Very well,' he said, agreeing to go.

His wife watched him gather his clothes into a small bundle. 'I'll bring you back a gift,' he said, adding, 'Tell no one where I've gone!' There was no embrace. He walked away in the company of the strangers.

The wife looked after him as he went down to the beach. There the white boat now rode at the lip of the filling tide. She saw him leap into the boat. She saw the oars cut into the deeper water. He turned his face upwards towards the cottage and half-raised his arm in farewell. When she saw that young Mary Mathias O'Sullivan from Gortadoo was also watching from inside her cottage door, Sibil Manning's face clouded with anger.

8

After a month or so Manning returned. At dusk his bulk darkened the doorway. He carried a sailcloth bundle over his shoulder. His deep-set eyes looked first at his wife's body. 'Aye, Limerick,' he said.

After a meal he began to speak. His story had to do with the marching of men, the clattering of hooves, and the windy snapping of banners. The treaty had already been signed when the French fleet tied up under the city walls. A great stone had been set up at the bridgehead to signify good faith. Admiral Renaud was contemptuous of the Irish officers whom he met returning from dinner with the Duke of Württemberg. 'The English will break the treaty before the ink with which it's written is dry,' he declared, adding, 'We have the ships, the stores and the men.' The Irish refused to break their word.

The standards of Europe were set up on a wide field at Thomondgate: Manning illustrated its width with his hands wide apart. The ragged soldiers of the disbanding Irish Army marched past, falling out of the ranks when they reached the standard under which they wished to serve. Most had elected to serve with France.

Embarkation began. The ships began to transport the soldiers downstream—Manning himself was on board the French flagship. Wives, concubines, sisters, camp followers tried to follow—he saw their hands sword-slashed from the gunwales as they sought to join their menfolk in the boats. The rejected women flung their infants after the departing vessels; they themselves drowned in scores as they tried to retrieve them. Men leaped from the ships to save their women. They too were lost in the swift-flowing river. The remnant left behind gathered in a doleful crowd on the quays. Clawing down their sorry rags from their breasts the women gave vent to a drawn-out cry of despair and anguish.

'Come to my cabin, Monsieur Manning,' the Admiral had said as the younger man prepared to leave the vessel at the mouth of Smerwick harbour. 'Look about you. What is it you wish to have as a souvenir? Gold, silver or wines? A necklace for your woman? A bangle? A ruby to remind you of the bloodshed of Limerick? A cradle—this? Oh, no! it is a coffer. See how delicately it is made. It is for whatever purpose you wish. It *could* be a cradle. It's big enough to hold an infant. Or your head, Monsieur Manning! Haha! Smell the wood. *Aromatique!* See, lined with velvet the colour of the lilac. How ancient it is I do not know. For your first-born? *Très bien!* It is yours. I shall have it wrapped in sailcloth. It shall not then attract the attention of a thief. Be careful as you go. There are spies everywhere. You have been of service. *Merci beaucoup! Au revoir!*'

As Manning unrolled the canvas, his wife waited, her lips apart in eagerness. He held the coffer on his palms, admiring its outwardly splaying sides, its ornamented lid. When he raised the lid, the lilac lining contrasted with the deal furniture of the kitchen. The woman's eyes lighted with pleasure. Her nostrils flared at the aroma of the wood. She took the coffer in her hands.

'What's it for?' she asked.

'It's for the child to be,' Manning said.

'Won't he soon outgrow it?'

'He'll outgrow it for sure, but that won't hinder my dream.'

'Your dream?'

'Yes! Every Manning infant, from now until the end of time, when the birth-blood is washed from its body, shall be wrapped in maiden linen and placed in that coffer.'

'Why so that?'

'For the neighbours to admire.'

'What else?'

'So that every Manning will remember that it was I who piloted the French fleet to Limerick.'

'Oho, my bucko!' the woman laughed as her man stamped around the kitchen. Then, his body sagging with weariness, he threw himself down on the *cailleach* to sleep as if he had been beaten or were drunk.

The woman polished the wood and brasses of the coffer. She removed some of the blue delf on the lower shelf of the dresser to make room for the French cradle. On a sudden thought she padded on her bare feet across the kitchen and looked out the small window. As she had anticipated, in the valley below, half-hidden in fuchsia bushes and barely discernible in the last light of day, she spied the face of Mary Mathias O'Sullivan looking upwards towards the cabin. The wife's face congealed in anger. Then it cleared in contempt. No one could rob her of her man now.

But rob her they did! A few nights later as husband and wife crouched above the embers of the dying fire the couple heard a noise outside. Manning came to his feet just as the door of the cabin crashed in. Soldiers seized him and dragged him off to Dingle. Sobbing, the woman followed until she stumbled and fell. She lay there for a long time before she rose and staggered back to cry out her tale to the neighbours.

Manning was hanged. His body was then quartered. A detail of soldiers brought the quarters west in a cart. The soldiers took with them a sledge, sea-stakes and iron staples: they staked the quarters of the body on the last crags above the sea and on the edges of four headlands. The head had already been spiked above the gateway of the barracks in Dingle.

Whenever Manning's wife looked out over the half-door she

could see the circling sea-birds. They were shrilling and quarrelling as they fought for pieces of her husband's flesh. Scraps that fell from the beaks of the gulls were dived upon by gannets.

The barony crouched in cowed silence. The dancers of the Flat Rocks below Manning's cabin did not gather as was their evening custom. The chanter and the drone of the pipes were silent. From time to time people dared to turn their eyes to the headlands.

9

A month passed. Hail flailed the little fields. Sea-water reared in fury.

Mary Mathias O'Sullivan of Gortadoo rose at daybreak, pulled on her red skirt, gathered her small shawl about her shoulders and crept about the house on bare feet. She slipped mackerel into an arm-basket and covered the fish with a bundle of rags and tow. There was a glare and stare to her eyes as she closed her cottage door behind her.

The girl looked in turn at the low sky above the torn sea, at the headlands, at Brandon, its peak sheathed in grey mist. She glanced upwards to the Manning cottage, then hurriedly made her way across the bogland that edged the sandhills. Picking her steps in the as yet wan light, she walked quickly but furtively. The little shawl was drawn tight about her features, her eyes were fixed on the ground. She staggered upwards along the pathway that led to the saddle-pass in the hills. Reaching the pass she paused to look down on the tall white and grey houses of Dingle where already the first smoke of morning rose from the chimneys of the thatched cabins set about the inner harbour. The masts of sailing ships by the pier swayed like a wood of peeled pines.

When she came within a mile of the town she drew aside to a roadside stream. Squatting, she rubbed mud to her shins and feet, lightly dusted her face with clay, then, taking the bundle of rags and tow from her basket she stuffed them up her skirt and blouse, holding them in place with a tight binder. She ruffled her hair, then smoothed it carelessly back into place. By this time her eyes, that up to this had been glazed with craziness, had lapsed into a normality of sorts. Entering the town by a high back road she slipped through the sleeping streets. She did not return the salute of the few whom she met on her way.

Reaching the barrack gate she looked about her, then ventured to look upwards at the head impaled on the spike above the crenellated gateway. It was the only head there at that time. Not that she would have had difficulty in recognizing the powerful skull with its deep eye-sockets, its features thinned to rust brown, its black tongue that idled forward from the mouth. An old woman coming out of the cabin across the road threw her a guarded greeting in Irish. Mary Mathias did not reply.

The girl knuckled boldly on the great wooden door. When the slot was drawn to reveal a pair of watchful eyes, '*Iasc!*' she said, indicating the basket of fish. The soldier growled at her in English: obviously he was telling the girl to be off. The shutter shot home with a thud. The young woman beat on the timber with her fist; when again the eyes showed '*Iasc don chistin!*' she shouted angrily and added a torrent of vituperative Irish. The word '*chistin*' sounding as it did like the English 'kitchen', acted as a password. Cautiously the soldier opened the wicket door.

High-pitched English is answered by guttural Irish. The woman, her rag-belly thrust out, is stabbing her finger at the fish basket. She is trying to brush past the sentry. With his left hand the soldier grips her by the throat, then looks down at the swollen body and the fish. 'They're not up!' he shouts, relaxing his hold and jerking his thumb in the direction of the cook-house. The young woman indicates her willingness to wait. The soldier cracks a coarse joke. The woman mock-smiles in servility as she slips past him and through the open doorway of the guardroom.

She glances quickly around the room. Her eyes flicker as she spies the opening to the left of the fireplace behind which is a door obviously leading by stone stairs to the roof. The soldier shouts over his shoulder as he slams the wicket, but the girl is already seated on the form inside. Entering, he finds her with her head bent and her legs spread. She is gasping for breath. She raises her hand to beg him take the basket of fish to the cook-house. The soldier gestures and shouts, bidding her to the errand herself. She gasps the more, then raises her voice in blackmail. There is a pause. The smell of whitewash, the smell of soot from the fireplace and the smell of fish lie heavy on the air. At last, with an angry shrug, the soldier snatches up the basket and hurries off.

Silence. The young woman lifts her head. After a moment of acute listening she pads to the foot of the spiral stairway, opens the door and begins to scramble upward. She staggers, clambers, blunders, crawls. At the head of the stairway above there is a low timber door leading to the roof: she struggles vainly with the wooden bar which holds the door closed until she finds out that the bar shafts its full length into the masonry at one side. The door opens, flooding the stairhead with light. Now she is out onto a valley of the roofs. Sunlight struggling through the mist of morning dazzles her so that she shields her eyes with her hand.

For a moment or two she is unsure whether to turn left or right. Left, she tells herself. Her hands rocking from sloping roof to sloping roof, she reaches a wall that rears above her—the crenellations indicate that it crowns the front wall of the gateway.

Just then there is a loud knocking at the main doorway below. Peeping down from between two crenellations she sees below her an old man with a donkey creel of turf. As she lowers her head she spies the white face of the old woman in the cabin opposite, her lips moving as in prayer. As again the turfcutter raps on the door with the knob of his crop, the voice of the returning soldier rings out bidding him take his time. The old man grumbles, then looks dolefully down at his shaggy ass. Mary Mathias O'Sullivan blunders forward, then upward. Above her, between her and the dazzle of the sunlight, she sees the head of Manning.

She claws upward, straddles the wall and, leaning forward on her cushioned belly, rides the topmost crenellation. Gripping the stone between her thighs, she raises her hands and lifts the damp, brown head, its hair matted, its cheeks fouled with bird droppings, its nose attenuated, its lolling tongue bearing a drop of morning mist at its tip, its ingrown eyes reduced to crusted slits deep within which sea-birds have appeased their hunger. As she draws the head towards her she almost loses her balance and comes close to falling to the cobbles below.

The old turfcutter, his mouth open, looks up, first in amazement, then in crafty understanding. Mary Mathias hears the loud voice of the doorkeeper, then the great gate below her creaks open on its hinges. The turfcutter, his eyes now firmly fixed on the cobbles, passes slowly in. He seems to be having difficulty guiding his ass forward. The doorkeeper yells at him to hurry.

Mary Mathias hurries too. She is back in the roof valley, she is through the little doorway, pushing it to behind her. She is halfway down the spiral staircase. At a slitted window she stops and raises the red skirt high on her breasts. She unwinds the soiled binder, then tears the bulge of rags from her body. She crouches and contracts her belly to receive the head. The features press on her bare skin. She tightens the binder so as to keep the head in place, then stuffs the sides with wads of the rags and tow. She shivers but not with cold. The rest of the rags she casts behind her on the stairway. Quickly she tugs the band of the skirt into place and drops the skirt about her.

At the foot of the stairway she crouches behind the door. She listens. She hears the returned sentry growling his puzzlement at her disappearance. She raises the skirt, spreads her legs and begins to pass water. The water trickles out from under the door and leaks on to the floor outside. Her waterflow ended, she listens craftily. The door is flung open. The sentry stands there, a look of incredulous disgust on his face.

Shouting the name of Christ he throws the basket from him. He lunges forward and grips the young woman by the throat. Mary Mathias mock-whimpers for mercy. Roaring his sense of outrage at the filth of Irish bitches, he thrusts her through the guardroom doorway. Dragging open the wicket of the main gate, he flings her headlong on the cobbles outside, slamming the wicket behind her.

After a moment of disbelief the girl staggers to her feet. Across the roadway the old woman standing just inside her doorway has placed her joined hands to her lips. She seems to be uttering sounds like 'Vo! Vo! Vo!' The girl tightens her shoulder shawl about her and staggers away.

Clear of the town she moves cautiously cross-country. Her eyes are fixed at intervals on the saddle-pass above. Her hands are pressed against her sides. Now and again as she climbs awkwardly over a loose stone wall it collapses beneath her. She tumbled into a bog pool: fouled with dark water and black earth she emerges to listen for sounds of pursuit. Satisfied that no one is on her trail, she resumes her upward staggering towards the pass. Gradually, the glaze of craze returns to her eyes.

★   ★   ★

A skein of young men and women drifted towards the piper's cabin. Two of them—a young man and a young woman—stood outside the half-door as a deputation of sorts; the others remained on the rough track above. The piper did not need to ask their errand: he pushed open the half-door and walked past them towards the ridge on which his cabin stood.

From there he could see three of the headlands on which quarters of Manning's body had been staked. Shading his eyes with his hand he looked at each in turn. The sea-birds had finished their work. He looked north to Manning's cabin which hung just above the natural platform of flat rocks on which the young men and women were accustomed to dance. The house was closed and appeared lifeless. He turned to read the attitude of the young people. They seemed to convey that there was an urgency in the bodies of the ready-to-be-weds that cried out for music and the dance.

The piper returned to the cabin and after a few minutes emerged with his pipes cradled in his arms. The waiting pair laughed: the girl turned to wave the good news to her companions above. Mock-dancing as they went the others began to move towards the Flat Rocks. Somehow the news spread through the townlands. Young men and women came hurrying. Arrived at the stone platform, the piper seated himself on his well-loved boulder.

Presently a skirl of music was in the air. It proved to be a tentative testing of atmosphere, which the musician quickly broke off. Then two groups of young men drifted to the centre of the dancing area. There, their heads together, they began to converse in low tones. After a time one young man looked over his shoulder and with a glance asked a girl to be his partner: she responded with a faint nod of acceptance. The other men found partners in the same way. As again the piper began to play, two groups of girls, each brilliant in a red petticoat, wearing a white blouse with crossed sashes of green or blue, joined the waiting men. The men wore rawhide pampooties, the women were barefooted. Thus, apart from the music, the dance was soundless.

There was a measure of defiance in the dance. Each woman conveyed wordlessly that no matter how powerful death's dominion, the time came when the passing of a man was irrelevant. It must then yield place to the needs of woman when she subtly conceals her desire, the while she plots to appease it. To the men the sweat-smell of the dancing women was as powerful as the fumes of hillside whiskey. In its traditional pauses and parts the dance moved to a swirling climax.

At the moment of climax the music faltered, then trailed off into silence. The dancers grew still: all eyes were on the musician who was looking down onto the lower ground. There the figure of a young woman could be seen staggering across the rough fields.

Querulous voices were raised: 'Who is it?' 'Is it Mary Mathias?' 'She's fallen.' 'She's up again.' 'Shall we . . .?' 'Keep away from her!' 'There's a cracked drop in the Sullivans.' 'I saw her at first light moving up towards the pass.' 'She's making for Manning's.' 'Only Manning's wife is above.' 'No love lost there!' 'Two heifers lowing for one bull.' 'She's staggering now.' 'She's at the door.' 'She's hammering on the door.' 'She's falling.' 'No, she's steady.' 'See how she grips her body with her hands.' 'She's like a woman that'd be on her time.' 'The door is open.' 'She's in.' 'What is it she's shouting?' 'That she's in labour?' 'Nonsense! Yesterday she was as slim as an eel.' 'Mary Mathias O'Sullivan is as mad as mad can be.' 'Quick, young women—while the door is ajar!'

In mid-kitchen in the Manning cabin, Mary Mathias wriggled and screamed. Standing in front of the *cailleach* bed, her eyes wide, the wife of Manning watched. Moving soundlessly, the young women tip-toed in. Mary Mathias's body movements grew more abandoned. She mouthed incoherencies. Seeing that the bed was denied her, she clawed at the deal table under the small window. She tried awkwardly to drag it towards her. A youngish girl broke from the watchers and helped her to push-drag the table to the middle of the floor.

Crazily Mary Mathias had begun to lilt the dance-tune that her coming had interrupted. Pausing in her lilting, she screamed that a dead man's head had fertilized her body. As if her madness were contagious, the young women took up the lilting. They began to move as in a dance. One or two men entered. Striding forward a man snatched a bundle of bogdeal tapers hanging beside the hearth. He threw them onto the embers of the fire. Presently the kitchen, in which, up to this, the light of the window and doorway had been cut off by the bodies of the newcomers, was lighted by erratic flames. The flames clasped the bulk of the iron kettle hanging from the crane and flickered on the petticoats of the women, on the delf of the dresser and on the clasps of the French coffer. The smell of blazing deal tanged the air of the kitchen.

By now the dance was more stylized—this though it continued to hold overtones of abandon. As, writhing awkwardly rather than dancing, Mary Mathias vaguely sought the table's end with her buttocks, two of the older girls gripped her by the shoulders and, bearing down on her, pinned her on her back to the surface of the table. Dancing and lilting pulsed and throbbed still more wildly. Then, two women, uttering animal cries, tore the skirt upwards from the recumbent figure and, quickly unwinding the binder, snatched away the rags and pads of tow. In a sudden cessation of sound and dance following on a hiss-like sigh, the head of Manning was revealed.

Fork-naked and spent Mary Mathias lay without movement. Her eyes were closed, her face was as pale as death.

Manning's wife walked slowly forward. As the women made way for her, the firelight played on the head, where, its features down-turned, it nested on the white thighs and whiter belly flesh of the girl.

Manning's wife extended her long bare arms. She took the rusted head into the cage of her fingers. She raised it slowly, then turned it over so that the features were fully in her gaze. She looked for a while at the horizontal slits of the eyes, at the distorted nostrils, at the pendent tongue. The head had thinned and fined: it was as if the dark features had been pickled by exposure to the sea-wind. As it took and lost the firelight, the face was seen to be aloof, stoic and self-contained. The woman brought the head to her lips. As with open mouth she began to caress it, the watching girls uttered she-cat cries. They clawed forward, their nails and finger-tips imploring to be allowed to touch the umber talisman, the more daring among them pleading soundlessly for leave to place their lips on the decayed features, or at least to stroke the soiled hair.

The smell of woman. The smell of clay. The smell of burning deal. The head that was an infant: the head that was a head. The tranced ex-dancers. The erratic firelight.

Still cupping the head in her hands, Manning's wife snarled at the younger woman lying on the table. Mary Mathias sat up, looked about her in an access of sanity and shame, dragged her skirt down about her, slid off the table and scurried out the door. As Sibil Manning gestured, someone poured hot water from the kettle into a china basin. She lovingly washed the head and dried it. She combed its hair. Again she gestured and one girl brought a square of virgin linen while another lifted the coffer from the dresser ledge and placed it in mid-table. As Manning's wife swung open the lid on its brass hinges and the wood smell rode over the death smell the watchers again yielded further light from the cabin window. The wife covered the padded lilac-coloured interior of the coffer with the linen cloth. On this cloth she laid the head of her husband.

Two old women, each bearing a lighting candle of yellow tallow, came through the doorway: one of the candles they placed at the head, the other at the foot of the table. Immediately, as on a signal, most formally swaying back and forth above and about the open coffer, the women, old and young, began to *caoin*. The sound of their 'singing' moved out through the open doorway and was heard in the cottages near and far.

As dusk fell people gathered into the wake-house.

10

The parish priest of 'Ferriter in that year of 1691 was a man called Éamonn Lynch. He lived in a tumbledown shanty in Ballynana and in the most wretched conditions possible. In that year of the War of the Two Kings a priest's head and the head of a wolf carried the same price-tag.

As a rule the priest read Sunday Mass in a mudfloored cabin west from Clasach. The cabin which served also as a Latin school and a threshing-floor stood, or rather sagged, in the middle of the bog at Móin Mhárthain. If the weather were dry a white gansey spread on a hillside bush indicated to the countryside that the Mass would be celebrated in the open air. Word was passed secretly to distant townlands and on Sunday morning people trudged over moor and mountain to attend. Sentinels were posted on high rocks to warn of the approach of soldiers. The altar was a natural rock close to Lios Mhárthain and was raised a little above the level of the surrounding bogland.

Since the day was fine the Mass of the Head of Manning was celebrated in the open air. All morning people streamed in from the ends of the barony. They came from Feohanagh and Bally-david, from Coos and Lateeve, from Fort del Oro and Kilmalke-dar. They came from the cliffs above Glenfahan and from the sand-dunes of Ventry. They came from Monaree, Curragraigue and Coumeenole. They came from the southern slopes of Brandon Mountain. Answering the waving shawls on Slea Head on the mainland, shepherds and fishermen rowed in from the Great Blasket Island.

There were thousands present when Father Lynch, wearing a scrap of black stole over his frayed chasuble, the poorly dressed chalice weighing down his trembling hands, his lower lip pendu-lous, his eye-rims brightly blepharitic in his chalk-pale face, shambled out of the scrub of Lios Mhárthain and squelched slowly towards the rock altar. The chalice rattled as it hit the stone. Then the priest turned and looked out at the congregation. Crossing himself he bowed in turn to the headlands of Fiach, Ceann Sraithe, Liúir and Páirc. He then bowed to the French cradle which rested on a smaller rock before the altar. Turning to address himself to the business of sacrifice he began to intone the Latin psalm.

Later in the Mass, after he had incensed the coffer and the four headlands afar, the priest turned and addressed the people.

'*A Phobail Dé*,' he began—'People of God, we are gathered today to celebrate a Mass with a difference. This Mass will be remembered among you and among those who come after you as *Aifreann an Chinn*, the Mass of the Head, since the head is all we now possess of the mortal remains of Seán Manning, the rest of his body having been delivered up to the fowls of the air and the fishes of the sea.'

The priest paused as seagulls mewed above him. 'But I tell you, people of God,' he went on in a strong voice, 'that what we have of this man is more than enough to ensure that his memory shall live on in the imaginative life of this locality. Today we skulk in the celebration of our mysteries. Today all we have left of a brave man is his head. Bury it proudly! Bury it ceremoniously! Bury it hopefully! It is a seed that shall come to a mighty fruition. You all know how he was betrayed into the hands of King William's soldiers by the Coonachawns of Graigue. But I raise my voice to tell you this, and let father remind son of it in the years ahead: the informer and his seed, breed and generation shall melt like

128

froth at the edge of the tide. And although Seán Manning was the only man of his surname to settle here among us and as yet it appears that he has had no issue, I tell you that, despite the barbaric manner of his death, the descendants of Manning shall yet be numerous in this locality.'

At this point Manning's wife, who had been kneeling among other women on a pad of hay in front of the crude altar, came to her feet. Throwing back her headshawl she began to cry out in Gaelic. She cried to the priest, then she turned to cry to the congregation. At first no one understood what she was saying but when she broke from restraining hands and moved forward to stand beside the French cradle and face the people, her words could clearly be heard.

'The moonblood of my body has not shown,' she shouted. 'The prophecy of the priest shall be fulfilled. Before God and the Mother of God these breasts of mine shall yet suckle a son of Seán Manning.'

The priest did not seem upset at the intrusion. When the woman had been led quietly back to her hassock, he resumed the saying of the Mass.

*　　*　　*

First came the priest, a white sash about his shoulder, helping himself along with his thumb deep in the fork of a thumbstick. Next came the piper. Next came the coffer borne in turn by a succession of nubile girls. Then came the thousands of peasant mourners.

The piper played *Caoineadh na mBan san Ár*—'The Lamentation of the Women over the Slaughter'—and when the cortège reached Dún Urlan graveyard the mourners gathered in a great circle about a neat rectangular hole cut deep into the sandy ground. As the priest recited the *De Profundis*, those present, the men clad in *báinín* frieze trews and pampooties, the women in black shawls and black petticoats, listened in silence. When the recitation had ended, the French cradle was passed around to be revered. The men touched it with their fingertips, the women kissed it and a young girl laid her cheek flat upon its lid. Sea-birds shrilled overhead. Waves broke to spume on the headlands of the Great Blasket.

At last, when the coffer was returned to the graveside, the linen-shrouded head of Manning was taken out and handed to the wife. Drawing aside from the host she parted the linen laps and spoke quietly to the head of her husband. She then replaced the cloth and, turning, handed it to two girls who were kin to her and who stood one on either side of the grave. These girls, kneeling on the grass, lowered the head into the slot in the soil. Men quickly shovelled sand on top of it, pounding the top sod into place with their heels. They were careful to scatter the remaining sand with a branch of broom so that the gravesite could not be readily detected. After the mourners had dispersed, the two girls who had placed the head in the grave took turns carrying the French cradle back to Manning's cabin.

One old fisherman with wild eyes and a crisp head of short grey curls remained behind. Confident that he was not being observed, he paced here and there taking careful bearings on the gravesite and aligning rocks, hilltops and headlands as he did so. This his great-grandfather had done more than a century before as the *Santa Maria de la Rosa*, a ship of the Armada, sank slowly in the Blasket Sound.

I I

The wild-eyed man who had told me the tale walked with me to Dún Urlan churchyard where many of its older graves had reverted to unmarked sward. There, pacing to and fro, muttering to himself in the evening light and taking bearings from fixed points on the coastline, at last he dug his heel into the sod. 'The head is buried here,' he said. Anticipating the question I was about to ask, he went on, 'Manning's wife gave birth to a son. That son in turn fathered seven sons and one daughter. As each infant was born it was washed, wrapped in clean linen and placed in the French cradle. There is no shortage of Mannings here today.' Then he strode off into the gathering dusk.

I needed time to adjust to these sensations so I continued to postpone my leaving the area. With each passing day there came the gradual awareness that the composite Celtic head I had hitherto imaginatively taken with me in my travels had merged wholly into the more powerful image of the head of Manning. The head too had become much more than a familiar of mine, for I recalled the traditional belief that whoever possessed the head also possessed its power. What this power or role was I could not as yet define but I was aware that at times it occasioned in me not merely revulsion and terror but something far more significant.

*　　*　　*

Day followed day deeper into a mellow fall. Day after day too I drifted on Smerwick beach, clambering up the heathery flanks of the hills or loitering in twisty boreens selvedged with blossoms fallen from the gorse bushes. What was I waiting for? I asked myself.

One day, I left the beach and plodded upward towards the dunes. The hills of sand were sweet-smelling; neither the grass nor the sandgrains about its stems made the slightest movement or sound. I was conscious of the male smell of the sea. I was conscious too of a certain inevitability like that of a woman moving towards a tryst.

Reaching the top of the highest dune, I surveyed landscape and seascape to ensure that I was unobserved. I paused to listen to a sheep bleating on a distant mountain flank and to watch a school of dolphins turning their black millstones as they passed the mouth of the bay. Having made certain that there was no one in sight, I stepped down into a small sandy hollow, its edges screened by marram tufts which lay just below the dunetip and to the landward side of it.

As I moved downward around the edge of the recess I was conscious of moving in a half-circle through the colours of the prism until I was enclosed in an off-white space below. Here, when I had eased myself flat onto my back on a bed of warm sand, I found that all sound was shut out, even the cries of sea-birds and the lazy hiss of the sea. I now had the far notion that I was no longer mistress of myself.

Closing my eyes, I began, slowly at first, to draw air through my nostrils, releasing it through my slightly open mouth. My finger-tips of their own volition began first to sift the sand, then to claw it on either side of my body.

Opening my eyes once to look up at the high flawless sky, I allowed

131

my limbs to slacken. Then, little by little, I yielded myself up to whatever forces within me had begun to clamour for release. Almost at once I experienced a deep pulsing accompanied by a sense of constriction. It was both a pleasurable and a painful sensation.

After a while I grew conscious of the exertion of soft pressures just below my ribcage on either side of my body. They could well have been caused by wads of rags or tow. I then had the feeling that the lower part of my stomach was firmly held by a linen binder. Later I could feel the press of strong cold features on the skin of the lower part of my trunk. I could clearly discern the jutting nose, the bold forehead, the determined cleft chin—I could even identify the place of the eye-sockets by the twin absences of pressure.

I was suddenly conscious of the lolling tongue lying just below my navel.

The pulsing ceased. It was as if I held a mighty breath, such as I had never held before. Somewhere above me, in power, rose and reared a primordial master. Whether sage or avatar, redeemer or lover I could not tell: all I knew intuitively was that for me he had come to put to rights a world askew.

Then, under a rhythmic compulsion, I found my body moving of its own accord. A minute part of my consciousness told me that for the first time in my life I was bridging the chasm between fantasy and reality. As the tempo of my movement increased I heard myself uttering a password, an incantation, an entreaty, a command. 'Manning!' I cried through clenched teeth and as I did so whatever consciousness remained to me reminded me of the pun implicit in the name. My lips twisted in bitter pleasure. Then, still more unrestrainedly, I cried the name aloud.

Then just as a mare is served, as a ewe is rammed, as a bird is trodden, so also was I manned, manned, manned. 'Manning!' I screamed through my coupled and clenched teeth. And even as the name issued from my mouth I could feel the masterful tongue-tip drawing closer to my womanly core. I continued to cry out, the while my back arched and the limb-flaps of my body opened and closed. I was overshadowed, I was parted, I was pierced. As in a dream I continued to scream until there was unheeded froth at my mouth corners and tides swilled and swelled, seethed and hissed in the inmost caverns of my body. 'Manning!' and yet again 'Manning!' I screamed until at last with a drawn-out cry of despair and release I fell back exhausted on the warm sand.

Compassionate Grounds

Is that you, Canon Tim? On holiday like myself—eh? My, but the red buttons suit you. A canon of the Cathedral Chapter eh? And me, your old classmate, still a country pastor. Well! Well!

Walk along the road with me. There's plenty of time before luncheon. Aye! I *am* lighter. I lost almost two stone early this year. And I never got it back.

A-a-a-a-h! That's wonderful sea air.

How did I lose the weight?

I lost it because of a harmonium, four swans, a Judy-the-Breasts, a school register, a silver-mounted claw, a dozen oysters, butter and honey, a minnow in a great lake and a claret waistcoat.

No, Tim, I'm not gone out of my wits.

Mind you, earlier this year I went damn near doing just that. For a while I thought my bishop'd have me locked up. Not a soul around? Good! Listen carefully.

As you know, after we were ordained, I served for a while in Scotland. Then I came home. Curacies here and there. For the past five years, however, I've been parish priest of a place among the Kerry hills, an area of middling farms between two tourist roads; call the parish backward or unspoiled, whichever you prefer. Emigration thinned it out. The village—the hamlet rather —has the usual church and a couple of pubs. I get up in the morning, say Mass, read the newspapers—if they arrive; I hear confessions and chat with the farmers—mostly about matters like the heifer subsidy. I've a late-middle-aged housekeeper called Janey, who's a good cook. I'm contented—rather, I *was* contented until I got the shock that almost killed me.

A-a-a-h! I need that air.

The parish school is a mile and a half uphill from the church. For all intents and purposes I'm the manager. It's in a townland called Tyreda. The lady teacher there is a Mrs Miriam Melton—

133

she's in her early forties and very aloof. She's really the assistant; her husband is the schoolmaster and teaches the boys, but everyone knows that *she's* the boss. Mrs Melton dresses in black. She has a frill down the front of her white blouse, and a cameo brooch. She plays the harmonium in the village church on Sundays. She has trained the girls from her school to act as choir. Mrs Melton's mother played the harmonium before her. And *her* mother before that again.

As well as running the school, this schoolmissus almost runs the parish. She collects the Christmas Dues. And the November Offerings. And the Oats Money. And the Stations Stipends. And the Famine-in-Africa money. She writes down an account of all parochial income in a notebook and gives me a balance sheet every half-year. And she never trades on her position. Even Janey, my housekeeper, kow-tows to Mrs Melton. And that's saying something!

Her husband, the schoolmaster? He's a genteel sprig called Matthew. Mattie Matchstick, they call him. Family? One girl in her teens.

Doesn't all that sound satisfactory? It does? Wait!

*   *   *

One frosty day, I whistled for my terrier. 'C'mon, Tara,' I said. 'We'll walk to the schoolhouse. We'll question the kids on the attributes of a glorified body—no joking, she tries to tell them all about agility, subtility and brightness.'

It was the 11th day of December. It was two weeks exactly to Christmas.

I went up the hill.

At the school, I shook hands with Mattie. 'She wants you, Father,' he said, in a strained tone. I walked into the other classroom.

Mrs Melton had a flush to her cheekbones. After the usual small talk she asked the girls to leave the room. She gave me the school register to sign. I signed it. She glanced from the open book to the attendance board on the wall.

'The Inspector was here yesterday, Father,' she began quietly. 'The average attendance is certain to be down for the current quarter. If the figure for the quarter ending 31st March next isn't up considerably, it will seriously affect my position.'

'Next quarter the numbers will rise,' I said smoothly.

'There are only two new infants of age to attend school. That's not enough to make a difference.'

'Now—now!'

'On April 1st I'll either have to agree to accept demotion or take a panel appointment. I cannot accept demotion.'

'This panel appointment?'

'I must take the first vacancy offered in the diocese. Or be dismissed.'

'Even if the vacancy is . . . in Caher?'

'Anywhere in the diocese!'

'I'll be in Dublin after Christmas,' I blustered. 'I'll settle that matter with the Department of Education. Make your mind easy!'

She looked at me with those steady eyes of hers. Through the glass partition Mattie's doleful eyes, too, were fastened on me. The girls in the playground were oddly silent.

Two days before Christmas, when the children were on holidays, I found Mrs Melton in the sacristy collecting the dues.

'Well?' I said.

'The numbers for this quarter are down.'

'Your family has given almost one hundred years of service in Tyreda,' I said stoutly. 'I'll see that you hold your position.'

She resumed her writing in the black notebook.

After Christmas, I was in Dublin. The Principal Officer in the Department of Education wore a grey conservative suit; he also had a grey conservative mind.

I explained the case of Mrs Melton.

'These regulations were framed in the interests of Department, managers, teachers, parents and pupils,' he said primly. 'If the average figures are down for the next quarter, Mrs Melton knows what that means.'

'Our diocese is eighty miles long,' I said.

The official pursed his lips.

'She plays the harmonium,' I said. 'And trains the choir.'

'She can leave the service and devote her full attention to these activities.'

I returned to my parish. 'It's complicated,' I told Mrs Melton. 'Next quarter will see everything right.'

New Year's Day came and galloped away. So did Epiphany.

One Saturday in mid-January I strolled as far as the school-house. Peeping through the window, I read the attendance board on the wall. The numbers were still going down.

That week I had an excuse to go up to Dublin. Reaching the city centre, I said a prayer in the Pro-cathedral. Then I trotted across the road to the Office of Education.

The Minister was away opening an exhibition of audio-visual aids to teaching. The laddo with the grey suit was attending an educational seminar in Cardiff. I was interviewed by a sniper of a clerk wearing a claret waistcoat. He had a nervous twitch to his nose.

'What's your problem, Father?' he asked.

He said this as if he were selling periwinkles.

As I told him my story his nose twitched sympathetically.

When I had finished, 'Try a fag, Father?' he said, with a glance at the door.

I told him I didn't smoke.

'She's handy around the parish?' he whispered.

'A treasure!'

'Zero hour 31st March?'

'Yes!'

He walked to the window. I could hear the organ playing in the Cathedral across the road.

'Is she ill?' the clerk stabbed.

'As healthy as a hound.'

'What age is she?'

'Forty-three or -four.'

'Husband alive?'

'Yes!' (I thought of Matchstick.)

'Children?'

'One—a girl—at a boarding school.'

As Claret Waistcoat came away from the window he glanced towards the doorway and then blew smoke down his gyrating nose. 'The fellow who framed that regulation thinks he's Fowler of *English Usage*,' he said with a snort.

He paced away from me. The light from a high window was behind him.

He turned. Did he chuckle?

'In confidence, Father?'

'In confidence.'

136

'If Mrs Melton were expecting an increase . . .'

'In what?'

'In family . . .'

I gaped.

'You could then make an appeal for her retention,' he went on, 'on compassionate grounds.'

I groaned.

'It's the best I can think of,' he said.

I hurried home. I sent for Miriam Elizabeth Melton. Shortly before she arrived, the post brought me a letter from the diocesan office.

There was one panel vacancy in a school in a benighted corner of the diocese, high in the mountains beyond Caher. A lake, four swans, water-lilies, rocks, a half-sunken green boat—I did relief duty there one summer and even then it was a penitential station. And Mrs Melton would have to stay at Judy Hanratty's . . .

'Please sit down,' I began, when Mrs Melton had arrived. 'I was in Dublin. The Minister was opening an exhibition. The Principal Officer was on holidays. I saw a bright young man. He wore a claret waistcoat.'

'Yes?'

'He said that if the average was down for the current quarter, the regulations seemed watertight. However—his personal opinion of course—he thought that a case for retention could be based on grounds of . . . health.'

'I won't pretend to be ill, Father.'

'You mustn't be *premature*, Mrs Melton,' I said, then winced at the word. 'He was speaking in the sense of . . .'

'Of what?'

'Of . . . maternity.' There was a long—*pregnant*—pause. 'But,' I said softly, 'that seems out of the question.'

Mrs Melton's brows knitted. She looked around the room. She then looked straight into my eyes. 'You mean that if I were . . .?'

'You'd be retained, Mrs Melton . . . on compassionate grounds.'

Her face was suddenly a screen behind which different emotions flitted in procession.

She came to her feet.

She looked steadily at the religious calendar on the wall.

'I'll . . .' she began.

If I were put on oath, I couldn't say whether she said 'I'll see about it,' or 'I'll try,' or 'I'll do my best.' In the hallway, as I was opening the door for her, I could sense that her ears were testing the noises of the house. Satisfied that Janey was not about, Mrs Melton said, 'I won't put you to the ordeal of discussing this with me again.' (Me! Ordeal? Confessions in the Gorbals!) 'but if God sees fit to . . . to send me another child, as I turn from the harmonium at the Gospel of the Sunday Mass I shall blow my nose with a lace handkerchief. Then you may be kind enough to write to the Department and tell them . . .'

'. . . that it wouldn't be advisable . . .'

'. . . for a woman in that condition . . .'

'. . . to be transferred to an isolated district . . .'

'. . . where assistance of an obstetric nature . . .'

'. . . might not be available in the event of . . .'

'. . . the premature arrival of . . .'

'. . . of a . . .' I stopped.

'Thank you, Father,' she said in an odd tone of voice.

The door closed behind her. I leaned against it to recover my breath. I was what Janey, my housekeeper, calls 'agitated'.

*　　*　　*

Now solve this mystery for me!

How did my parishioners get to know all that had transpired in absolute privacy between Mrs Melton and myself?

And how did I know, the instant I set foot in the pulpit the following Sunday, that *they* were all aware of it?

And that *they* were aware that *I* was aware that *they* were aware?

Neither of us two main protagonists had said a word. And Matchstick was too timid even to breathe it. As for Claret Waistcoat in Dublin, it was as much as his job was worth to open his beak. And if Janey had eavesdropped it was contrary to all my experience of her.

And yet there in the pews was the full knowledge of our predicament as plainly as if each member of the congregation had seen it headlined in the local newspaper.

Let me utter another parochial profundity.

In every parish in Ireland there's at least one reformed ram.

By ram I mean a retired roué who sired a few by-blows in his lusty twenties, feared the climate of the United States and stayed at home to thump his repentant craw into a semi-righteous old age.

My repentant ram is called Taddy. He is now almost eighty. His ebbed vitality has its final lair in his bright eyes.

So, from the pulpit on that Sunday as I glanced discreetly at Mrs Melton seated on the harmonium stool and then involuntarily checked back to Taddy, his eyes carried my eyes one pew to the left to where Matchstick was sitting. By raising one eyebrow Taddy semaphored that, in this context, he reckoned my influence with the Almighty not worth a tinker's damn.

That wasn't all.

Taddy's eyebrow also hinted that that Judy-the-Breasts of his could maybe solve the crisis—that bloody stone statue that broke Father Brabazon's heart and the heart of every pastor in the parish for the last fifty years.

For, as a younger man, Thaddeus had found two pagan fertility images buried in a bog. The less obscene of the two he had surrendered to the National Museum and got his photo in the local papers as a benefactor of culture. The other he hid in his hayloft. After that he played havoc with the morals of the parish by showing this abomination to generations of courting youngsters.

I saw Mrs Melton look from me to Taddy. Her cool eyes implied that Thaddeus was simply a prurient little boy who had soiled his breeches.

*　　*　　*

February came in. The spring days passed in shining procession. Each Sunday, on entering the pulpit, I ran my eyes over the heads of the choir girls gathered around the harmonium. Sunday after Sunday I sought in vain for the flutter of a lace handkerchief.

Meanwhile, Mattie Melton's face had grown long. His red nose had an edge to it. There was a feverish spot on each of his cheeks. You'd almost have to crouch to see his eyes.

I began to feel the strain myself.

First, I lost my appetite. Mealtimes found me pushing the food around a plate. Janey prides herself on all kinds of cooking: land food, sea food, sky food—so she got as mad as a hatter with me. 'What's wrong with you?' she asked. 'Nothing!' I snapped.

She didn't speak to me till the following Sunday. I noticed then that she heard Mass, not in the sacristy as was her privilege as priest's housekeeper, but in the nave of the church.

There she sat, her eyes boring holes through Randy Taddy, Mattie, Mrs Melton—and myself.

* * *

Let me, this sane August day, try to view the matter objectively.

A school with a falling average. A teacher-organist lost. A routine problem you'd say.

If nightmares were routine, I'd agree.

I'll not mince words. With every day that passed, the devil began to torment me more and more as once he tormented Our Lord high over Jerusalem.

I found myself mentally yelling at Mattie Matchstick in an unseemly way. Worse still, I even wanted to push Mattie aside as a man unequal to the feat demanded of him.

This is serious, I told myself in my more lucid moments.

But what led me to exculpate my soul—and this exculpation came barely in time for the preservation of my sanity—was my remembrance of what Dr Thomson, the professor of moral theology, had once said to me in his study in Maynooth.

'In you, sir,' he said, 'the competitive spirit is hyper-developed. If it were unbridled ambition or common lust, I would be concerned with your future as a shepherd of souls. But it is not that. For you, life is a race, a chase, a dealt hand of cards, a pound bet on an outsider, a pair of cockroaches racing for the hearthstone. Your passion is for hooshing on the most decrepit nag in any race in the forlorn hope that it will win. Watch that weakness, sir!'

With the passing years I had mastered this gambler's instinct of mine. And now, here it was again. A race in progress, the winning post approaching, the spectators crowding the pewstands —all was brandy in my blood.

Humour helped to ease the situation for me.

I saw Mattie Matchstick as an angler with a naked hook, fishing wildly for the single minnow of a human life that darted hither and thither in the shoreless lake of eternity.

* * *

March came bursting in; there was a quickening of Sunday tempo. When, in church, a hymn broke out from the knot of girls around the harmonium, I found myself being dragged along in its wake. Janey had settled in the nave as if for life. Randy Taddy had his arms folded tight across his chest. The face of Mattie resembled the back of a fiddle painted white.

'I'll never last!' I told myself with a groan.

*　　*　　*

One Saturday night as I left the church, weary after having heard long-winded confessions, I found Matchstick waiting for me near the presbytery door.

'Someone sent me oysters,' he whispered. 'By post.'

'Who?'

'I don't know.'

'Tck-tck-tck-tck!' I said.

On St Patrick's Day the last of the spring daffodils stood on the altar. The singing of 'Hail Glorious Saint Patrick' sent the congregation and myself up into a spiral of excitement. After the Mass, the melancholy strains of 'God of Mercy and Compassion' (*compassion*!) cast us down and gave us all the holy-willies.

By this time I was living on one slice of toast a day. Shaving, I had almost to fill my mouth with mashed potatoes so as to get the blade to my cheeks. Janey seemed poised to mount a broomstick. A fortnight to go, I told my glassy eyes in the mirror.

All this time my parishioners had been digging, metaphorically, of course, their elbows into my ribs. In the course of a harmless chat at breakfast in a farmhouse parlour, after I had said Mass in the house, I passed some idle remark.

Taddy immediately leaned forward. 'What grounds have you for saying that, Father?' he asked.

Grounds! Everyone collapsed in laughter. And after a time-lag the damn peasantry in the kitchen took up the cackled chorus.

*　　*　　*

This year, if you recall it, the feast of the Annunciation fell on the last Sunday in March. With us, by long tradition, the eleven o'clock Mass on Annunciation Day is invariably a sung Mass.

Queen Bee and her handmaidens were at the harmonium. Mattie Melton sat in a pew-corner like an old cock canary in a breeding cage. Janey. The Ram. Hoi polloi.

The first narcissi were in the brass altar vases. Spring spoke with the voice of a bud rubbing sensually against the glass in a leaded window beside the pulpit. It was the time of the annual agony of the celibate.

As I had expected, the church was crowded; a shower earlier in the day had been seized upon as a parochial excuse to wait for the later service. Some of the latecoming worshippers were standing at the doors or were down on one knee by the walls of the aisle ('ecclesiastical fowlers taking aim at Almighty God,' Father Brabazon had called them), their eyes glittering above the bitten peaks of their caps.

This parish is out of its mind, I told myself. First chance of a change I'm off like a redshanks.

Spiritually speaking, I am now on turf that quakes beneath my boots. And yet, the closer one goes to absolute sanctity, the closer one is to blasphemy.

Knowledge of this anomaly was what had caused the flesh to peel from my bones. For I dimly saw that I was dealing with an odd kind of holiness—the only kind of holiness that my parishioners understood. For if I were to talk to them about metaphysical attributes or mystical bodies, about Teilhard de Chardin or neo-humanist manifestos, they would all groan inwardly. But mating and birth they comprehended: the service of a valuable mare, a cow losing its unborn calf, a sow farrowing by lantern-light, these they understood and, by their standards, reckoned holy.

As the time of the Epistle and its subsequent Gospel drew nearer, I found myself trembling with excitement.

After the Collect I chanted '. . . world without end . . .', listened to the chirped 'Amen' from the little choir, then turned to walk to the lectern to read the Epistle.

All were seated. All were silent with what I quickly realized was a silence touched with sadness. A man scraped in his throat. Mrs Melton's choristers stood ranked beside her. The mountings of her brooch flashed. Her hands were joined demurely in her lap. Her eyes were downcast in her pale face.

I stood there suddenly afraid.

The words of the Epistle of the day met my eyes. To me they

seemed the prompting of the Holy Spirit. I began to read aloud the Lesson from the Prophet Isaiah:

'Ask a sign of the Lord . . . either unto the depth of hell or unto the heights above. Achaz said: "I will not ask and I will not tempt the Lord . . ." '

(But I asked . . . and I tempted the Lord.)

'In those days the Lord spoke to Achaz,' I continued . . . 'Therefore the Lord himself shall give you a sign . . . Behold a virgin shall conceive and bear a son and his name shall be called Emmanuel. He shall eat butter and honey . . .'

And so to the end of the Epistle. From the pews came the final loud response: 'Thanks be to God!'

'The Lord be with you!' I began again.

'And also with you!'

'Continuation of the holy Gospel according to St Luke . . .' I said.

All rose. The schoolmistress in the midst of her choir. The housekeeper. The old womaniser. The matchstick husband. The worshipper-spectators.

I began to read:

'At that time the Angel Gabriel was sent from God into a city of Galilee called Nazareth to a virgin . . . and said unto her: "Hail, full of grace, the Lord is with thee, blessed art thou among women." Who having heard was troubled . . . And the Angel said to her: "Fear not, Mary . . . behold, thou shalt conceive in thy womb and shalt bring forth a Son . . . the Holy Ghost shall come upon thee and the power of the Most High shall overshadow thee . . ." '

I paused.

Over my glasses I saw the set faces of my people. As again I raised my voice I was conscious of inching closer to the core of a great blaze.

I took a deep breath and read:

' "And behold thy cousin, Elizabeth, she also hath conceived a son in her old age . . . because no word shall be impossible with God . . ." '

Whereupon, from her sleeve, Miriam Melton took a small hand-kerchief, edged with light lace, and unequivocally blew her nose.

Had the Angel Gabriel blown his trumpet, it couldn't have had a more powerful effect on the congregation.

The eyes of the girls in the choir took me most. I'll go closer still to the truth. When we men are face to face with something incomprehensible, there is a tendency on our part to fall back on vulgarities.

Meanwhile, below me, the tension had grown to the proportions of an over-inflated balloon. But the face of the schoolmistress was tranquil.

'Dearly beloved brethren,' I began with a great effort, 'let me preface my homily with a few words that are relevant to the text from Scripture I have just read for you. I had thought it would be my sad duty today to tell you that the mistress of Tyreda school would be transferred on April 1st. As a result of intelligence just received, I am happy to announce that by the intervention of Providence she will be with us for many years to come.'

Ever hear people cheering in church?

That damn rascal Taddy led it.

My ape of a housekeeper was crying. Mattie Melton was grinning like an idiot child. But that incipient harem of girl choristers never even looked sidelong.

Looking back on it now, I'd swear that the girls had known of it in advance, even without being told, and that Mrs Melton had silently charged them by the dignity of womanhood not even to hint of it in the presence of vulgar males.

The remainder of the Mass I said as if I were a chamois leaping from rock to joyous rock.

The harmonium began its rattling and wheezing. Then the girls raised their voices in a hymn that had triumph and thanksgiving to its echoes.

* * *

Taddy and Matchstick were waiting for me outside the church. Janey, too, was standing a little to one side.

Taddy, I saw, was slavering with delight.

'In pre-Christian days,' he began, 'the Irish people had a wisdom all their own . . .'

'There's substance in sea-food,' Janey snapped.

' 'Twas God that did it!' I said sternly.

'And man, too!' Mattie said in a voice cracked with indignation.

As we all laughed together, I thought of Claret Waistcoat. There and then I offered a fervent prayer that God would cure him of that nervous twitch of his nose.

The Right to be Maudlin

Gradually I came to learn the dimensions of my impending loss —the length, breadth and depth of it. It was only this morning that the telephone rang to tell me of the retraction—up to now the possibility had been a vague terror, a wild animal, as it were, locked away in a cage of my mind. I was dimly aware, of course, that once released its capacity to maim and maul would be immense. But that was all.

Since the phone rang and the message has been conveyed and received, nothing is the same. Nor will anything ever be the same again! For now there is definition and intensity. Sights, sounds, smells, tastes and, above all, sensations of touch are sharply outlined. And no matter how earnestly my innate sense of charity pleads for an understanding of her who has retracted there remains a part of me that screams my utter conviction that something that is mine and mine alone is being wrenched from me. And because of this sense of offence and outrage, I claim that, as a woman, I have earned the right to be maudlin.

There were times during the past five months when I was truly happy. Happy in the natural routine the acquisition of the infant had imposed upon my day and night. There were the chores I found so pleasurable, the small rhythmic offices of attention that afforded me such a keen maternal delight. I found myself able to set aside the knowledge that in its essence much of my happiness was vicarious, and still relish the novel fact that after so much waiting, each minute, hour, day and week had meaning.

So, as in their sum the weeks, adding up to a month, recurrently told me that I had passed yet another milestone, I experienced a sense of relief: this relief, however, was soon replaced by the gnaw of anxiety, for there was still the sense of a winning post ahead and the fear of a nameless rival behind.

I knew that if I managed to remain in front at the final post in this six-months race against time, no legislation on earth could have snatched the boy from me. Not even the natural mother, whoever she was and wherever she was, could then claim a hair of his head. But now I am forced to come to terms with the grim awareness that almost at the moment of victory I have lost the race against time and the powerful forces of law and nature.

During this period of uncertainty, a gestation of the nerves as it were, marked by alternate moods of gloom and elation, I did not sleep properly. Sleep, I kept reminding myself, was a luxury that could be postponed until all was secure. The ringing of the telephone invariably struck terror into my heart. And it was ironic, or fitting, or perhaps inevitable, that during the last week of all the telephone had shrilled with what seemed to be a cumulative stridency so that before lifting the receiver I paused to bid myself be calm, to reassure myself that everything would be normal, to recall once again the conversation I had held long-distance with Mrs McArdle, the social worker, only three days ago.

'How is he?' came her first query.

'Fine!' I answered.

'Thriving?'

'Thriving by the minute!'

'Good!'

'I've had him out on the lawn for the past few days and he's as brown as a berry.'

'I bet he is, what with all the fine weather we're having.'

'You'd love to see him now, Mrs McArdle! Everything all right at your end?'

'All is calm; all is bright.'

'Thanks be to God. Another week and I can relax.'

'I think you can relax now.'

'I'll try! If you should pass this way in September . . . Or Father Seary, if he is free, either one of you, or both, will be most welcome to spend a night or two with us. Paul and I would love to see you again.'

'Thanks for the invitation.'

'We've loads of room, and a big empty house.'

'Not so empty now!'

'That's true. I'm looking out through the glass of the patio door. I can see the pram with the sunshade tilted over it—this side of the privet hedge. I wish you could see his bare legs cycling in the air.'

'Good!'

'Be sure to tell Father Seary how things are with us here.'

'I will indeed—you'll have to excuse me now. Someone has come into the outside office.'

'God bless you both! And thanks for everything.'

That call brought me minor relief and a brittle sense of elation. This morning's call was different.

*   *   *

The day began as usual. A delightful end-of-summer morning. The baby had had a night of unbroken sleep. At breakfast there, as usual, was Paul behind his newspaper and, later, hurriedly wiping a drip of boiled egg off his chin before driving to the office. 'What a messer,' I told myself with a smile. I was looking forward to teaching the baby to wave goodbye to Paul when he was leaving. Apart from the upstairs noising of Nora Joe, the maid, the house was still. Then the telephone rang.

My hand paused before taking up the receiver. A few seconds later, I heard a strained query in my ear. It took me a moment or two to recognize Fr Seary's voice. After a non-committal phrase or two, 'Muriel,' he said in a quiet measured tone, 'I'm afraid we have a retraction problem here.'

'What does that mean, Father?'

'I'm sorry to say that the mother wants the baby back.'

Father Seary is a young man. He goes on to tell me that this is the first time he has had a retraction. In the Adoption Society one could go for years and not have one. He couldn't tell me how sorry he was. *She* had turned up, and was fully aware of the six-months clause. And she was to marry the father of the child. After the marriage the couple were taking the baby to New Zealand. It was all arranged. The priest understood how emotional it was for everyone concerned. Actually, the mother had come into the office while Mrs McArdle was speaking to me on the phone a few days before. Mrs McArdle was really upset. If it suited they could travel down on Monday—that would leave the baby with us over the weekend. But, yes, if I wished to get it over —a sword hanging over me—they could go down today.

'Come today, please,' I blurted. Would I phone back when I had spoken to Paul? Was I quite sure there was no need? Yes, he and Mrs McArdle would leave immediately—within the hour. The very first time it had happened! It was a consolation that the couple were to be married. If only I could see how happy they were. It was out of the question that Paul and I meet the mother. At that moment the natural parents were waiting at a house in the suburbs. Together waiting for the baby—yes. *They* had suffered too. The girl had had to tell her mother that it wasn't a holiday abroad. No, I wasn't to prepare a meal. Mrs McArdle and he would have lunch on the road. It would take about three hours to get here. They would be here about 3.30 or 4.00 p.m. and leave again as soon as possible. Would I prefer it if he phoned Paul? Very well. He'd leave it to myself. The priest asked God to love us both very dearly indeed.

The receiver fell out of its cradle twice as I tried to replace it. I looked around me.

I was conscious of a wider territory having been staked out so as to enclose me, an area within whose confine I would have the right to be incoherent, unrestrained or maudlin. I have a thing about being maudlin: it has to do with Madame Pierre, Superior of the Convent of Les Filles de la Sainte Mère de Dieu in Cheltenham, in which I spent five years as a school boarder. It has to do with Madame Superior's warning pupils against being maudlin as a means of defusing pent-up feelings. She was adamant on that, was Madame Pierre.

To myself I say, Now that I am wounded, how dare life move on! How dare traffic shuttle past our white front gate! As if nothing were amiss! From the nursery with its nursery rhymes on the wallpaper I look out at the privet hedge, at the brown legs cycling in the air, at our spiky cairn terrier asleep under the pram. I look about me. The giant panda—there he lolls in a corner of the room, a gift from the Spina Bifida Committee of which I am a member —the Secretary brought it with a note of congratulation. There, too, are the silver christening cup, the pink rattler, the soiled napkins in the nursery bucket—no matter how stained they were, to me they were beautiful—the tins of baby food, the mock teats, the sterile bottles, the pale blue cot, the Moses basket, the ABC book, the carry-cot, the car-chair, the feather-light quilt, the butterfly net of the pram hood, the small gaudy picture of the

Virgin I meant to hang inside the baby-car, the ribbons pink and blue and mauve, the emollient jellies, the tins of talcum powder.

I resolve to bundle them all together and throw them into the car as it is leaving with the child. I ring Paul.

'Paul!'

'What is it?'

'Please come home at once.'

'Is it . . .?'

'Yes, please, I want you to leave this minute. Sit into your car and come back immediately!'

'I'm leaving.'

'Hurry! Phone your father and mother. *They* must know. I'll tell Claire myself. The baby is to be taken today—I decided that was best. Hurry!'

'I'll be with you in a few minutes.'

Paul is Paul. He will acquiesce. His training as an accountant will help him to overcome his grief, to accept acceptance as an expression of social etiquette. Or does he feel at all? I keep hoping he will break. If he does, I may discover a deeper Paul and such a revelation may leave me a residue of value. The Old Missus is predictable. She will make damp conciliatory noises. The will of God. All for the best. Divine Providence. The ways of the Almighty are not our ways—she speaks in proverbs and murmurs pious invocations. The Old Boss is different: he can be dangerous. At this moment he may be putting a bottle of whiskey on his head and could arrive here like a grenade. My sister Claire, once I phone her now she'll drop everything and hurry here. She'll smoke cigarette after cigarette, non-stop, from now until the baby is gone. Suddenly I think of Nora Joe, the maid.

Once the baby came, Nora Joe, defiantly, almost surlily, tried to take over the care of him. It was as if the mystery surrounding the child's origin had the effect of multiplying the girl's affection. Alone with the baby, her stolid features are transformed. Spying on her I have wondered at the change. Her expression shifts quickly when anyone enters the room. So, like everyone else, Nora Joe wears a mask. Telling her will be an ordeal, but it should be something of a rehearsal for me, so that I can better cope with the others.

Time? Let me see. They should be here about three-thirty in the afternoon. It will be a tiring journey for them—here and back on the same day. Yes, I realize that they will be eager to turn around and be off as soon as it is decent to do so. I'd better have some sandwiches ready. Yesterday's roast is in the fridge. I'll send Nora Joe for a coffee cake, an almond log and some confectionery. There are rock buns in the bread bin. I'll put out the blue teaset and the best cutlery. The hand-embroidered cloth with the scalloped edges. The silver tray and the Wedgwood cakestand. The trolley perhaps. Claire, as always, is certain to bring an apple tart. Cigarettes and apple tarts—these are her standbys.

'Nora Joe! Sit down a moment. I've just had some upsetting news about David. The six-months probation period isn't up until the fifteenth of this month. The final papers would have to be signed before that date—the papers giving him up. And now the natural mother, the real mother that is, is being married to the baby's father, and she wants her baby back. They both want their baby back. The priest and the lady from the Adoption Society will be here in the afternoon.'

'They're takin' the child, ma'am?'

'Yes.'

'Today, ma'am?'

'Today.'

'How can they do that, ma'am?'

(Steady now! I tell myself. I'll have enough to cope with without having a hysterical girl on my hands. If Nora Joe took it into her head to grab the baby and race across the field towards the river, I wouldn't have the strength to stop her. We'd have a scene then with the whole suburb looking on. The Guards would be called in. All the details in the newspapers. Perhaps a case in the lawcourts. Steady now!)

'The mother *has* the right, Nora Joe.'

'She gave up her child, ma'am. How can she have a right any more?'

'She could take back the right within six months. That's what she has done. It's the law.'

'The word 'law' causes the maid to pause. I am quick to take advantage of her hesitation. 'Like a good girl, run down to Dalton's. Get some cakes, and a dozen assorted confectionery. Here's the money. Off you go!'

Dulled, dazed and on the edge of revolt the girl leaves. As she goes she looks down uncomprehendingly at the treasury note in her hand. I too am a little dulled and dazed. I find myself going over the events of the past few months.

* * *

For Paul and myself this was our final chance of a child. We had long since wearied of consulting gynaecologists. Besides, we were both almost forty: beyond that age applications for adoption were unwelcome. We had debated the matter for years. On reflection I seem to have debated it aloud—with myself. Paul had listened. Had nodded pseudo-sagely at the proper moments. Had gestured vaguely where a gesture was called for. Had finally agreed quietly. The influence of his acquiescent mother superimposed on his professional training had made him what he was. Invariably, when in the course of business he sensed that a client was determined to pursue a certain line of action, he knew how to acquiesce with grace.

For all that, walking into the Children's Hospital must have been a bewildering experience for Paul. For me, it was the greatest adventure of my life. A child was to be born to me. The gestation period was long and painful—even if it had existed only in the womb of my imagination. Perhaps it was all the more real because of that. Seated with Paul in the hospital waiting-room, with the cries of infants remotely reaching us, I found myself in mental labour. I listened acutely. Did one infant voice cry 'Me!' above all the others? I twined my fingers in my lap: I knew that for the adoptive parents there was no element of choice. I recalled the voice of Mrs McArdle saying, 'We *do* try to match the environments of natural and adoptive parents.' And the voice of Father Seary murmuring, 'Confidentiality is total, you understand?'

We had requested a boy. And then the white door of the waiting-room had opened and hey presto! there in Mrs McArdle's arms was the boy. I was given him to hold. I uncovered his face and looked at him for a long time. I looked up into the faces of the others. No help there. If a mistake was to be made, the fault was to be mine alone. There followed the gentle testing of limbs and on my part a sidelong head movement to see if the child's now open eyes would follow. I recall some mention of rudimentary tests of intelligence.

At last we were—I was—faced with the decision. I had reserved the right not to go ahead if I took an instinctive dislike to the child. Now, with the infant in my arms, I found my emotions naked. I was reduced to intuition alone. Again I looked up into Paul's face. Still no guidance. His mouth corners conveyed that it was my function as a woman to choose, his as a man to approve. I asked for time to think matters over.

We went out to a café and drank coffee. Claire joined us. We said little that was relevant to a decision. As we prepared to leave I looked directly at Paul and said, 'All right!' On our return to the hospital, Paul seemed reluctant to go in but did so when I insisted. In the waiting-room I signified our assent. 'Mine!' I muttered fiercely as, with the baby in my arms, we made our way into the open air. The others told me later that during this ordeal I had betrayed no traces of emotion. If this were so I must have been hearing the voice of Madame Pierre. As I tightened my arms about the infant I fancied I could see her lips curling with contempt for anyone who betrayed emotion: '*un spectacle en pleurnichant*' was how she phrased it. So my gait was steady as I walked to the car.

We named him David. This was for the Old Boss, Paul's father. The old man thanked me with his dark eyes. Paul, as ever moon to everyone's sun, was pleased because his father was pleased. Paul's mother was pleased because her husband and son were pleased. Watching us four, Claire, her spinsterish eyes shifting from one of us to the other, inhaled more deeply on her cigarette.

Once the baby was installed in our newly built house the building had come alive. It assumed a personality. It became noisy. And it smelled. I experienced initial distaste for, as a child, I had been reared in an atmosphere of asepsis.

*   *   *

Tonight the house will revert to its former lustreless self. The process already appears to have begun. The tassels of the parlour blinds that wagged quite merrily this morning now depend as if taken by a sullen fit. As momentarily the sunlight fades, the dull glint of the chandelier conveys dejection.

Outside, however, it is a perfect late-summer day. The baby air-cycles merrily on. The cairn is scratching his back against the undercarriage of the pram. Where shall the visitors sit for tea? I hope the Old Boss and Old Missus will sit down with them.

Then 'Paul!' I cry out as he enters the room.

And even as his arms are around me and I quietly quell the temptation to blubber, there is a distraction. I look over his shoulder and ask myself in the name of heaven what is the meaning of the cavalcade of autocyclists already halfway up the driveway. My hands fall to my sides. I remember that it is the party of American students come to camp in our lower meadow. I quite forgot that Paul had given them permission through the local Junior Chamber of Commerce.

'Here they come!' Paul, obviously relieved at the diversion, opens the french window and raises his voice above the noise of the thirty machines to speak to Declan Connors. 'Lead them right down. Tell them to set up at the lower fence. They'll find running water in the yard!'

They pass the window, riding in pairs, boy matched with girl, fine-limbed young men and women moving in purring procession before Paul and myself, the coloured tyres spurning the loose gravel of the driveway. Their faces are set, as if they have come from a different planet, yet under the helmets the young women's faces break into restrained smiles as they pass the sunshaded pram. Spikier than ever, the cairn comes out to investigate. He is unsure whether or not to bark. From the pram, his feet stilled in the air, the infant listens, the machines continue to pass, each carrying a tapering steel rod attached to its front fork. At the top of each of the rods a pennant of blue and gold silk is alive in the movement of air. The wind-cheaters the students wear are orange and blue and red and violet and green. When the last autocycle has passed, I turn listlessly away. The room is heavy with silence. Paul continues to look out the window.

I now begin to explore the notion that there was a part of me never convinced that the boy would remain irreversibly mine—ours if I wished to be accurate. And on acknowledgment of the truth I spy through the window the figure of a red-faced Nora Joe returning with the cake-boxes. Has she told the neighbours? Have they read her agitated movements? And as this thought crosses my mind I see halted at the gate the dusty car with the Old Boss and the Old Missus clambering out of it. Invariably the old man, ever since he knocked over an ornamental urn on the edge of the lawn when reversing, parks his car most awkwardly at the outer gateway. 'Go out and meet them, Paul!' I say. Paul obeys at once.

As he goes, I sense that a dam has built up inside me, and that I must be on my guard against the breaching of its great wall.

Step after step the old couple advance on the house. Paul walks to meet them half-way up the drive. I hurry upstairs. After a quick shower I put on a mauve skirt with matching blouse and a string of pearls. Then I stand at the window and look down on my disintegrating kingdom.

The Hondas are silent, yet the muted cries of the students come erratically from the meadow, where their coloured garb is vivid against the aftergrass. Two cream- and orange-coloured tents stand out while the pennants on the stacked machines contrast with the darker green of the woodland across the narrow river. An Indian summer if ever there was one! Nora Joe wheels the pram to the back of the house. The Old Missus follows her. I spy down and watch the pair looking tearfully into the pram, then Paul's mother draws aside the cover on the now sleeping infant. Somehow I am extra-conscious of my body as I step down to embrace and be embraced by the old lady.

'A cup of tea?' I ask the Old Boss, addressing him through an open window.

He is toeing a large coloured ball on the patio. He wakes as if from contemplation and growls a startled 'No!' The ball has scurried away from him: he looks at it stupidly for a moment or two, then, as if resolved to abandon it, moves towards the white lattice of the fence. He tugs sharply at a tall grass stem; when it breaks he taps his forehead with the loaded seed-head. The kettle boils. I wet a pot of tea. Paul sits deep in an armchair in the sitting-room. He pretends to read a newspaper. Claire is here now, her face blotchy. She makes appropriate sounds, scuttles out the back door, then quickly returns to retrieve her handbag and to move upstairs.

The natural mother, I keep asking myself as I move about my chores—has she already seen her baby? Or, after the birth, did she order that the infant should be taken out of her sight so that later there would be no puckered-up old man's face recurring in her dreams? Or is this contrary to the nature of woman, no matter how intense her sorrow? The name and identity I gave the child will now be erased. This is good! I am determined that for me the parting will be as clean as the incision of a surgeon's scalpel.

But yet again, although I know that in the late afternoon the boy will move out of my life forever, I cannot help wondering whether out of some deep reservoir of instinct I would recognize him if I chanced upon him a grown man. Would he possibly turn out to be the young self-conscious doctor wearing the white coat and the stethoscope who has come to examine me as I lie dying? Would he, in unaware irony, leave my bedside to deliver a fatherless child? Would I start on seeing a picture of him in the newspaper, a footballer leaping high for a ball? Or would I, with a sudden wincing of the heart, recognize the face of the criminal staring out at me from the report of the murder trial? If I should chance to meet him on a social occasion dressed in evening clothes would I, an elderly woman, be tempted to say quietly, 'For five months you were mine, limbs, head, trunk, black hair, brown eyes, stubby fingers and toes. You belonged totally to me. It was my nipples wet with baby food that you, my surrogate son, sucked so determinedly. It was I who laughed when you were lying naked on the table after your bath and your small member stood comically erect to send an arc of urine into the air, taking me totally unprepared. Now you are a poised young man whose strutting betrays your consciousness of the nearness of the girl in the pale green evening gown. But I remember you weak, puny, parentless, your cry for recognition reaching me through time and space.'

Minute by minute, hour by hour, the day advances. Nora Joe has sidled off to her small bedroom off the kitchen, the Old Boss standing out of doors by the fence is dully watching the students setting up the smaller tents, the Old Missus is drying kitchen ware, Paul is opening and closing his roll-top desk, Claire has descended to the sitting-room and is punching cushions, the child is asleep and I, having piled the baby's clothes together, am now laying out tea things in the dining-room where Nora Joe, hearing the noise of delf, has just joined me. Everyone in his or her fashion is striving to normalize an abnormal situation.

Time turns the corner of noon and begins to slide down towards the inevitable. A perfunctory luncheon is eaten. Nora Joe eats in the kitchenette, her movements interpreting the process of eating as a treason of sorts. Whenever a motorcar stops outside the gateway we all cease our mechanical champing and listen, relaxing only when we learn that the alarm is false. After the meal Paul goes down to the stream at the end of the meadow farthest from the student encampment. The Old Missus has one eye on the front gate. Some of the students are filling their polythene vessels from the tap in the yard. I look again at Paul who is standing at the river's edge: wearing polaroid glasses he is trying to discern trout beside the swaying weed on the bottom.

'Ah!' the Old Missus says. We know at once that *they* have arrived. She adds in concern, 'Our car is in the way!' 'Leave it!' I snap. I'm now being devious: for some reason I want the priest and the social worker to leave their car on the road-edge outside. This, possibly, because already I look forward to the final rite or ordeal of taking the baby in my arms and walking out along the driveway to the road outside. For me this will be a walk of defiance, for in this newly-built suburb we incurred silent resentment by buying two of the riverside meadows in addition to the site. We are all new here, 'a mixed bag', Paul's father keeps saying, thus implying that few of the men are in professions and that the womenfolk haven't been to an English finishing school run by French nuns. Nor has any woman except myself a master's degree in arts! Perhaps there is a far more basic explanation for my insisting that the car remain where it is—I simply wish to keep out the brigands. And this, I concede, could in its turn be my first move towards exercising the right to be maudlin.

Fr Seary is an athletic young man. He grabs his jacket from the car and shrugs it on. As he strides purposefully into the driveway he is seen to be wearing a light-weight black shirt. I gather, even at that distance, that the shirt has the type of collar into which he can slip a strip of white plastic and thus transform himself from layman into priest—like instant tea or soup. Behind him bounces Mrs McArdle in a blue summer dress. She is ample-bosomed and middle-aged. With every step she indicates her acceptance of sorrow, hysteria, body emissions, cauls, breech births and birthmarks.

I walk to the front door. I smile my welcome. Mrs McArdle I embrace. I offer a limp hand to the priest. 'How are you, Father?' 'How are you, Mrs McArdle?' I slide them deftly into the sitting-room. 'Please sit here, Father. And you here, Mrs McArdle. You must both be very tired. It's quite warm today. As you say, an Indian summer. A tiring journey, down and up in one day. You've had luncheon? You might care to wash first? First right, first left. Excuse me for a moment. Nora Joe, go down to the river and tell the Boss come up. And wheel in the pram by the back door when

156

you're coming back. Claire, please! Don't fuss! Just go in and say, "I'm Muriel's sister." Don't stand there, Nora Joe! Just tell the Boss they're here. Let the Old Boss alone for the present. Off you go!'

Later: 'Try the cake, Father. The almond log is rather good. Sandwiches are sustaining. Scones, Mrs McArdle? The blackcurrant jam *is* homemade. Of course, Father, I understand. It is emotional, for everyone. And you are to marry them? Right away? How nice! Claire will be offended if you don't try some of the tart. And the baby's grandparents will be there, all four of them! Yes, indeed, joy to their hearts. And the young couple—they're going to New Zealand—at once! That's consoling—New Zealand! I appreciate their good wishes. And just now they're waiting for David . . . for the boy? Is that you, Paul? You both met when we were . . . up. I'll pour out a cup for you, Paul. Are you sure you've had enough tea, Father? And you, Mrs McArdle? Claire and Paul will see that you are not neglected if I leave you for a few minutes, just to make sure that everything is ready.'

'Nora Joe! I'm taking the baby upstairs for a few minutes. Don't sulk, please. Whatever happens, I am not to be disturbed. By anyone! Make any excuse you like. Hand him to me now. Better still, stand on the landing.'

'Hello, little man! Up we go! Up, little sleepyhead. You are with a woman who is tempted to exercise her right to be anything she pleases. In we go—right in here to the bedroom. Now to turn the key in the lock behind us. Here we are together. I'll put you down on the bed so that when you are fully awake you can kick to your heart's content. Kick and stiffen and smile. That's it! There you go, small fella. That's a big yawn. The best of friends must part. It was too good to be true. You are being . . . called away. I'm not sure what relationship I bear to you now. Proxy mother, foster mother, deposed mother or deluded ma? A university degree gives one the capacity to define. But for a line or two on paper we two would have grown old together, on the beach, in the street, in the woods. Up and over, son, till I strip you, as the Old Boss puts it, "to your pelt". That's it—growing older together. You watching life, I watching you. I would have rejoiced at your successes, grieved at your failures. I would have been amused at your first attempts at love. (Christ, *ma Mère*, the circumstances *are* extenuating!) Dear eyelashes, dear eyebrows, dear eyes! Dear limbs, ankles, navel, spine, nape of neck, poll that my palm cups. Fingerpads mine, don't dare forget your now sensations in the years ahead. A line of a song keeps running through my mind—"My fingertips remember you with joy". Lovely nut-brown boy, you will not now be buried at my side. Your wife will not now call me Old Missus, nor Paul Old Boss. Look up at me. Here is my open mouth about to blubber down on your flesh. Open mouth, don't you dare forget. Pointed tongue, play your part.'

I could cover my weals by reciting the blessings of the souvenir shops: 'As you climb the hill of good fortune may you never meet a friend.' 'May you be in heaven half an hour before the devil knows you're dead.' 'That the dust from your carriage wheels may blind the eyes of your foes.' 'Land without rent to you, the woman of your choice to you, a child a year to you—and death in Ireland!' This kind of stuff is mostly for export. Not for me! All I know now is that I'm human and a woman.

'That's all, son. In your short life you have made people very happy and very sad. That about sums it up. So, for the last time, with my open mouth on every part of you, I wish you luck. And I say goodbye.'

'Nora Joe, come into the bedroom. Close the door. Take him from me now. Thank you for sharing him with me. You'll get over it, girl; sixteen is a beautiful age. Cry if you want to. You and I are in the Bible. I'm Pharaoh's daughter finding the infant in the reeds. You are my handmaiden. I'm also the woman who lied to Solomon and claimed that the baby was hers. "How beautiful with shoes are the feet of my beloved." Cry, young woman, cry! If only *I* could cry, it might help to make me a natural mother. I feel like screaming when they talk about contraception and abortion. I was looking forward to Christmas and to seeing the candlelight on his face, his eyes on the lighted tree. In a way it's lovely to be hurt. That's all, Nora Joe. Give him to me now. Don't let them see that we're upset. Be sure to put the panda in the car. The other things too. Leave nothing behind. Run out now and tell the Old Boss that they're ready to go.'

★   ★   ★

'Father, before you leave you must meet the Old Boss—Paul's father. You'll take him gently? He explodes once a year. The baby was named for him. Paul is his only child, I'm sure you'll understand.'

'There you are, Sir? This is Father Seary. Father, this is Paul's father.'

The priest's eyes reach the sad mad brown eyes in the parchment of the old features. Last hope of perpetuation gone! 'And this is Mrs McArdle, sir. They must be off now. They're anxious to be back before dusk. Yes, they've had tea.' Mumbled words about weather and journey.

That much is over, without an explosion. Old-fashioned courtesy has won. The old man turns towards the pram in the hallway just outside the sitting-room door. Runs his knuckles down over the infant's cheek. Mumbles, 'Good luck, son.' Turns away. The Old Missus watches him narrowly.

'I'll take him to the gate, Mrs McArdle,' I say.

The baby in my arms, I begin to walk along the driveway. The infant is dressed in all his finery. I hear the cries of neighbouring children at play. Father Seary is a step ahead: his car keys jingle. The cairn terrier sniffs the air of departure. Mrs McArdle, the empty carry-cot in her hands, walks almost abreast of me. Behind us Nora Joe brings a load of baby things, surmounted by the great panda. The Old Boss and the Old Missus, the cairn between them, stand just inside the overhang of the porch. Claire watches from an upstairs window. Paul brings up the rear of the procession. Three pairs of American students, boy matched with girl, purr up behind us on their machines. Young gods, young goddesses— we pause to let the pennants and gleaming metal pass. They bow their helmeted heads in thanks—they pock-purr out and after a pause at the gateway flow fluently onto the main road.

As we reach the embrasure of the gateway, the priest hurries forward. He snaps off his jacket, folds it and places it on the back seat of their vehicle. He slips off the collar strip, opens the car door, and pushes his rump behind the steering wheel. Mrs McArdle places the empty carry-cot beside the folded jacket. Nora Joe is loading the boot. She still holds the panda. I gesture Mrs McArdle into the passenger seat in front and, standing at the open rear door, indicate that I am about to place the baby in the basket. I pause.

I am now conscious of the neighbouring women having drifted towards their gateways. I do not even know their names. Some shield their faces behind the low branches of shrubs or trees. The infant still in my arms, I turn right and left to acknowledge their presence. They lower the branches and show their faces. They wear slow sad smiles of understanding. The Old Missus, the terrier following her, has come out of the porch and stands a little distance up the driveway. She too must be acknowledged. I lean forward through the open rear door and place the infant in the cot. His eyes wide, he continues to look up at me. I fold the handle of the rattler, then, thrusting my hand down between my breasts, I take out a jeweller's box lined with green velvet. I verify that the box contains the sovereign. As I tuck it down beside the boy, I indicate to Mrs McArdle what I am doing (Victoria Station, I tell myself, as I recall the play). Nora Joe hands me the panda: I place it sitting on the priest's jacket. I close the car door and wish that the windows were less dingy. I go to the open front window and kiss the priest. I go to the other side of the vehicle and kiss the social worker. Then I stand back on the pathway.

The priest looks into the side mirror. He is seeking a break in the traffic which keeps pelting past. Belatedly Paul tests that the doors are fully shut. As the engine revs up we all call out muted goodbyes. Our fingers twinkle. A remote wave from the priest, then the car eases away. The panda has begun to sway. The neighbouring women allow their half-raised hands to fall to their sides. They continue to stand there, their faces semi-shielded by shrubbery.

*   *   *

Is my bedroom door securely locked from the inside? Is the house totally silent? Deliberately now, I will commence to rage.

I will tear off my clothes. I will throw myself here and there on the bed and on the floor. I will also peel off layer after layer of my conventions. Coldly and with deliberation I will deliver myself up to fury and hysteria.

I will attack the wardrobe, the mantelpiece and the dressing table. If those below have sense they will pretend not to hear. I know the terminology of foulness, the many names for the genital organs, the vernacular words and phrases for coupling. I can mimic the moans of a woman in labour, the screams of orgasm, the outraged yells of rape. 'Hear ye!' I cry. 'Hear ye the voice of a woman emancipated! Hear ye the growlings of a bitch whose pup has been wrenched from her teats!' Before Christ, I'll make this room dance so that henceforward it shall cower before me whenever I enter it. I will smash, shatter and break, tear, ravage and rend, yelp, blubber and scream. I am Magdalen in heat, Magdalen rampant, Magdalen denied, Magdalen maudlin. As Jesus is my witness there shall be no apologies, no explanations, no expressions of regret. If they dare to obstruct me I will claw them down. I am a woman possessed of an inalienable right. It is my only way forward—to balance, to normality, to lustre. To the utter fullness of womanhood.

Layer after layer is torn from body and mind so that now I stand erect in the white mansion of my skin and within the cold flame of my essence. Smash, shatter and break. Moan, yell and howl. Through profanities and blasphemies I sob my thanks to the nuns who dammed my emotions. Meanwhile, writhe, sway, seethe, bay, rave and wreck. Rage and again rage! Rage and vent the radiant obscenities that I have harboured and treasured and nursed against the transfiguration of this single fucking hour.

Island Funeral

As the throb of the trawler's engine reached the island, middle-aged women wearing black shawls and red petticoats came hurrying from the rocky uplands, from the hissing fields beside the dunes and from the low-lintelled stone cottages by the shore. The island pub disgorged its gulping customers while from the Gaelic summer school in the village hall boys and girls came clattering out in an issue of abundant colour.

There was a pause: then the older men came wearing homespun waistcoats and blue ganseys over voluminous trousers below which moved rawhide shoes of *úr-leathar*, coloured as the hide of the cow is coloured. Then a dark flock of Christian Brothers moving most discreetly was joined by a Swedish artist dressed in white and wearing gold-rimmed spectacles.

Last of all came the handful of summer visitors; ill-attuned to holiday mourning, they loitered, thus indicating their uncertainty in the matter of funeral protocol.

A woman of the island had died in childbirth in a Galway hospital. She had left behind her a husband and a young family of nine perched on a rocky shelf, there to face the world in an extremity of puzzlement that was more piercing than any sorrow. For how in God's good name could the mother fail to return now, as ever before, with her slender body, on her renewed legs, tongue-busy, seeking out what had happened during her absence, her ears alert for the subtleties or evasions of reply that betokened small domestic tragedies—a prized breakfast cup smashed, a well gone dry in the finest summer since the year of the English, a hen taken by the fox, a chicken carried high by a hawk, a kitten trampled upon by a pony or a boy nipped by a mad devil of a donkey?

Puzzlement—that was it. To the nine children, the eldest fourteen, a mother seemed as constant as the sun. So, for the woman not to return, not to walk, not to talk, not to love, not to be loved in return, not to bake, not to admire, not to grow exasperated, not to cuff, not to tie shoelaces and bows, not to crack clock-beetles under the shoe sole, not to lead family prayer at evening, not to rule, not to guide forever without foreseeable end—that was like the quenching of the sun itself in the island sky.

*　　*　　*

The faded blue trawler thrummed closer. Its bows carried an old colonel's moustache of foam; dark figures loitered on its deck. Four currachs offshore had broken off their fishing and had begun to converge on the point where the larger vessel would presently draw up beside the now crowded pier. As the trawler approached, a dirty tattered flag at its stern was seen to be flying at half-mast.

The engine of the trawler eased down and the vessel nosed to a gentle but ponderous rest beside the flight of slimy steps leading upwards from the water. Those above crowded forward to the sandstone pier-edge and looked down at the varnished coffin; the men below standing about the coffin looked mutely up.

The waves chuffed against the grey pier wall and against the jet rocks. The currachs drew alongside the trawler and, having made a rough-and-ready pontoon bridge by cursorily lashing the canvas craft together, their crews clambered on to the trawler's deck, where they shook limp-dead hands with the limp-dead hands of the men already on board. Eventually all the men on the trawler formed a knot, irresolutely looking down at the coffin.

No one spoke. The island stragglers continued to arrive.

From the trawler's deck men stepped on to the slippery steps of the pier and guided the bright elongated box upwards with seemingly awkward but accurate clutchings and palmings. Descending the steps, others clawed at it, finger-tipped it or lingeringly caressed it, until at last it reached the horizontal above, where, for a few moments, it was almost hidden by the bodies of the eight men standing upright—four holding it on each side.

An old woman now came forward. Ritualistically her hand emerged from under her shawl. She placed her palm flat on the coffin lid and, obedient to her implied command, the coffin moved soundlessly down until it came to rest on the floor of the pier.

163

With unhurried movements the old woman knelt beside it, spread her fingers upon its lid, brought her mouth down to the breast-plate, kissed the name printed in black on the metal and then, dry-eyed, began to *caoin*.

Other women approached and hung above her, crouching over the coffin and swaying in the antiphony of lamentation. Other women, too, not quite so close to the central scene, kept mauling their faces in the recesses of their shawls.

As on a signal, the dead woman's children began to cry in a different tone to that employed by the older women. Meanwhile, their eyes on the ground, the men became still more stolid.

Abruptly the old woman kneeling by the coffin ceased her lamentation, rose to her feet and, still dry-eyed, withdrew her face into her shawl. The crying of the children petered out into silence.

Six men raised the coffin to their shoulders and with a kind of natural sway the funeral began to move off.

There was no sound as the cortège passed across the edge of the sandbowl of the island. The sand rose in a low-hung fog that coated boots, slippers, petticoat ends and trouser tips with a dust as fine as boric powder. Struggling along the rocky pathway that led upwards to the church, the bearers sweated. The sweat could be seen glistening as it gathered behind their ears; later it fell in generous drops from sea-reddened lugs.

At the door of the church the boy-priest received the coffin. The salt-sea wind had eaten the tongue off the church bell that hung greenly in its detached belfry so that, although the bell itself swung dutifully as a boy drew on its rattling chain, the metal itself gave out no sound.

The bearers came to a halt as holy water from a dipped palm branch flashed in the sunlight and ran like mercury along the varnished coffin lid. The priest read invocations to which he himself responded in a slightly different tone of voice. The psalm read, he turned inwards towards the church; following him, the bearers, crouching so as to avoid striking the lintel of the door, entered the white-washed building.

Thundering in, the mourners filled the narrow nave. The coffin was placed on the pews on the gospel side and at right angles to the altar. When at last there was comparative peace in the crowded church the priest recited a rosary decade in Irish. The people growled reply. '*Aifreann amárach ar a deich; sochraid ina dhiaidh,*' he then announced. 'Mass tomorrow at ten—funeral afterwards.'

For perhaps ten minutes after the priest had left the altar no one stirred.

Presently, a toe-cap noised on the floor. Other toe-caps came in tentatively. A salvo from the toe-caps then indicated that it was time to go. All present rose and went out into the butter-coloured afternoon.

Evening came. A sun of copper ferocity set behind the sister island to the north-west. Afterwards there was an interval of in-between light; then an autumn moon appeared above the cut-out hill that carried a ruined castle and a Martello tower on its indigo ridge. Gradually the bowl of sand that lay behind the foreshore dunes became suffused with hues of grey and violet.

Devoid of far-carrying laughter, the darkened island at last grew silent.

★　　★　　★

Morning came with choppy waves slamming the beach; there was a breeze that set the noses of the sheepdogs smelling the land wind for rain. But no rain came; the normal sun again appeared and with its appearance the wind died. Again a trickle of people came streaming off the stools of stone that horizontally branded the hillsides. As the hour of Requiem Mass drew near the trickle became a stream as again the islanders poured into the airy, lightsome church.

The priest read the Mass. The psalms were not very poignant; it was as if the islanders instinctively realized that ceremony has as its purpose the reduction of chaos to order.

During the Mass the bereaved children remained ranked in the pews beside the coffin. They conveyed the impression that they had come to accept as a gift the shining coffin that had been given them and which, more's the pity, their relatives would presently hide in a hole in the hill of sand. So, after the people, led by the next of kin, had received Holy Communion, the tragedy for the children did not appear to bring with it any great measure of devastation.

The rites at an end, the visitors left the church first. The same six men who had borne the coffin the day before again raised it to their shoulders; led by the priest they moved out through the doorway, again crouching a little as they made their way into the sunlight.

'Is it right for us to attend the funeral?' a young woman visitor whispered in Irish to an islandman.

'Why not?' came the sharp reply.

'It might look as if we were treating it as a spectacle. The relatives and the island people might want the funeral to be private.'

'Death is not private,' came the sharp reply. 'It belongs to you and me and everyone.'

'Very well, so!' the questioner said. Tying a scarf about her hair, she joined the mourners.

The priest walked in front of the coffin. The spread-out people followed in silence. The coffin was shouldered down into the bowl of sand from the surface of which the wind had scoured all trace of clay and grass. The sand-powder again rose in a cloud that floated face-high; the downdrag of the sand beneath their boot-soles and the choke of it in their nostrils caused the bearers to slump and stagger. Snorting their vexation they struggled to hold their balance. Their movements were akin to a dour defeated swimming. Thus the cortège moved through a wired-off alleyway through the government-sown plantation of marram grass.

As the pathway ended, the bearers unexpectedly came to a halt. They lowered the coffin to the sand at a point where legend had it that an old church dedicated to Saint Paul once stood.

As the coffin touched the ground, the stragglesome zig-zag of people, its black elements lighted by blobs of petticoat-red, threw themselves sprawling on to the sand to pray. Kneeling, they experienced in full measure the violence of the midday sun.

The signal given by the priest, and the stop now prosaically interpreted as a welcome respite for all, the bearers came staggering to their feet and again raised the coffin to their shoulders. Each man dug his boots into the sand and spaced himself so as to ensure that he would not trip any of his comrade bearers. Then momentarily, and as a unit, the bearers paused to glare almost directly upwards at the churchyard on the dune-top, its crudely arched gateway and its awry crosses hazy in the shifting sunlight.

Sweat pouring down their faces, their necks strained like cords, their boots sliding, the men fought upwards. As one pitched sidelong on the shifting sand, the five others dug doggedly in until he had recovered his balance. The last twenty or thirty feet seemed agonizing for the coffin-bearers, yet no one in the cortège seemed vicariously to suffer, except perhaps the girls of the summer school who had demurely tagged on to the strung-out procession at a point close to the island hall. The young priest moved cautiously ahead, his cassock implying patient command.

Diagonally up and across the shellstrewn side of the dune the bearers struggled until at last they moved in under the arch to the point where, silhouetted against the sky on a hillock above an open grave, the priest waited. Beneath him in the centre of the cemetery dune, and below ground-level, was a sand-scoured church ruin where all night long on the eve of the feast day of their patron saint, with lit candles in their hands, the praying islanders kept vigil.

With a last dripping of sweat on to the coffin lid the bearers set their burden on the ground. Below the coffin the open grave darkened to dampness as it deepened. Panting secretly, the bearers waited for the rest of the mourners to arrive.

The cortège, with the Brothers as a black belt about its waist and its peacock tail of students still in the sandbowl, could be seen drawing itself slowly upwards.

Outlined against the sea a donkey attempted to nibble at grass where no grass grew. On the edge of an outcrop of stone two horses suddenly taking fright raced off in the direction of the island pump. The pewter-coloured face of the sea was marked by the black shape of a canoe and the orange buoy of a lobster-pot. Beyond the houses to the north-west the third island was barely discernible in the heat haze.

At last the priest began to read. Taking a bottle of holy water from the boatmaker's creosote-soaked hand, he flicked the mouth over the grave and on to the coffin lid. At last he gestured the end of prayer.

Sand from the grave edges having slid into the pit, two men leaped down and gestured to those above to hand them shovels. This done, they began to cast the fallen sand upwards. On the ground above a man gave curt orders in a tolerably loud voice. Others gave quiet prosaic directions. At last the grave was to everyone's satisfaction.

On a finger-gesture from the priest the men began to lift-slide the coffin towards the grave mouth where the pair standing in the grave received it. Now the hitherto anonymous husband of the dead woman began to cry out. Implicit in his cry was a violent anger. A woman, obviously his sister, wearing a black shawl and a red petticoat, tugged fiercely at his elbow and clucked at him as one would cluck at a refractory child. In his turn the mourning husband tugged his elbow fiercely away and continued with his angry cries. A pregnant shawled woman caught him by the other elbow; tugged this way and that, he continued his angry lamentation. For a time the children looked up uncomprehendingly, then, having interpreted their father's cries as sounds of sorrow, they joined in the mourning.

At last the coffin lay prone at the bottom of the pit. Standing at the head of the grave the man in charge gave orders to have the coffin shifted first to the right, then to the left. The nickel screws were now unfastened and laid on the coffin lid. The two men in the grave were pulled up to ground level.

The priest took a shovel and cast down three shovelfuls of sand.

As the first shovelful beat on the coffin lid the husband flung himself on his knees, lowered his head against the grave edge and there, striking his forehead against the ground, his buttocks upturned, his whorled crown of hair visible on his closely clipped poll, he wept and raged unrestrainedly. Meanwhile, the grave-diggers having begun to fill the pit, the pelting sand began to evoke resonance from the coffin lid. The husband still writhed in helpless anger. After a time, the priest, having handed his shovel to a bystander, bent down and most delicately placed his hand on the man's shoulder. The husband suffered the hand to lie there while he continued to beat his forehead against the ground.

As the pregnant woman now broke into unrestrained weeping the sister of the bereaved husband continued with valour to battle against open sorrow. To the last she kept tugging at her brother's elbow; time and again she drew him back from the edge of animal grief. Meanwhile, almost inaudibly, the children continued to mourn.

The resonance of sand falling on the coffin lid gradually decreased, and, long before the sand had drawn level with the grave edge, the sound could scarcely be heard. Under the tightening fingers of the priest, the husband, his features sweat- and tear-stained, shambled to his feet and looked dully down. As the heaping sand was thumped by the back of a shovel he gave a final cry which was answered by a cry from the pregnant woman and as quickly followed by a last upbraiding cluck from the second woman, and finally a short outburst of grief from the children.

After this there was no more lamentation.

Meanwhile, here and there in the graveyard, men sprawling on hummocked ground had begun to converse quietly. Secretly some of the younger ones had lighted cigarettes and the smell of cigarette smoke drifted among the mourners.

At last, with the grave heap trimmed, the priest indicated an end. The children looked up into their father's face. The man raised his eyes to look over the sea at the distant smoke of the city where his infant was still in hospital. He dried his face with the lining of his tweed cap, swiped it on to his head and, followed by all, moved away.

The people rose from the corners of the mounds and began to go out by the gateway. As they slithered down the side of the dune, limpet shells cracked and broke under their soles. As if the crackling had reminded him of something the husband stopped below the gateway and gave a last look upwards. Then he allowed the two accompanying women to lead him away. The children followed in a compact school.

The priest shuffled after, his head low on his breast. The Swedish artist remained on the dune top, his head at an odd angle and his face upturned to the sky.

A Woman's Hair

On Sunday afternoons when the bar was closed and my father had gone off to a football match my mother would take the opportunity offered by the quiet house to wash her beautiful hair. There were times when she would do so, I realized later, solely to gratify me, her only daughter—and indeed, her only child.

When my mother's hair was washed, rinsed and had almost dried, I would insist on her sitting on a rocking-chair. I would then stand on a stool beside her to catch the cascading hair above the point where it had gently tangled and would resolutely force the comb through it. As accurately as I recall the texture of my mother's hair, I also remember my stolid father's uncomprehension of it as a bond between me and her: all he seemed to understand was the filling of spill-over pint-glasses for the cartmen and countrymen who made the vacant lot at our gable on the town's edge a stopping place on their way to the market.

But always between my mother and me, and complementary to the bond of flesh and blood, was the shining spancel of hair. I combed it and plaited it and piled it and experimented with it until my fat father bustling in and out of the kitchen scarcely knew whether to laugh or to scowl at such tomfoolery which—to him—was of a piece with my mother's obsession with music and the incomprehensible tock-tock of the metronome on the top of our piano. And when, as ladylike as she had lived, my mother died, I was left with the memory of her hair spread out like a fan on the white linen pillows on either side of her waxen face.

After my mother's death—I was then ten years of age—I was packed off to a boarding-school. I pined for home and after two months was brought back and sent to the local convent day-school, where I was an irregular attender, being kept at home on slight pretexts.

At this time I was something of a day-dreamer: washing ware

at the window of the scullery, I would look out on to the vacant lot beside our house and watch the carters unyoke their horses and tie hissing nose-bags of oats about the animals' necks. I recall seeing a thunder shower fall on an unprotected box-cart of unslaked lime so that later the rocks of lime bubbled like molten lava. At certain times, too, the site grew still more interesting, for it was a halting-place for the restless of the Irish roads— umbrella-menders, ballad-singers, knife-grinders, men and women subject to the compulsion and tyranny of movement.

*　*　*

One Saturday evening in early January, as dusk fell, a tramp and his wife—more likely his 'woman'—pitched a crude shelter just below our scullery window. The ice-cold air and the early evening stars had already given warning that a night of heavy frost would follow. The shelter was a crude one—a dirty canvas sheet slung over a ridge-pole held three feet above the ground by a few curved sally rods with limestones fallen from our yard wall to keep the soiled skirt of the camp in place. The shelter could be entered at either end, simply by groping back the flaps.

The tramp was black-bearded and was sixty if he was a day; the woman seemed to be in her early twenties. She had clear-cut features with a weather-worn complexion and there was in her stare a vacancy that seemed to offer a clue to such an odd pairing.

But it was her luxuriant dark hair that, despite its tangled and even filthy nature, attracted my attention. It appeared to be of a finer texture than my own hair, or indeed than that of my mother, but the wind and sun had played havoc with it. I grimaced at the thought that such hair seemed a waste on the young woman's head.

As darkness fell, the tramp and his woman entered our bar, squatted on the floor in a corner, and began to drink stolidly, now and again muttering gutturally at each other. My father kept growling half-refusals to their requests for more drink, but the tramp and the woman kept blackmailing him and begging for more. I felt that my father continued to serve them simply because my mother had always pleaded for the 'travellers': 'Don't judge them, Tom—their life is hard. If they get drunk itself,' she would say, 'what harm is it? And they haven't far to go when they leave us—only from the bar to the gable outside.'

So, aloof and alone, the oddly-matched pair drank and muttered and growled and lisped and never spared an upward glance for the other customers.

When closing-time was called, and overcalled, with my father hanging threateningly above them, they at last staggered to their feet, bundled themselves out the door and moved towards their shelter. There, swaying giddily, they groped at the flaps and at last fumbled in, and down, almost bringing the canvas about their ears with their blundering movements. Watching them from the darkness through the just-open window of the scullery, the night air icy on my face, I wondered at the mystery of the cave in which they slept, with perhaps their bodies oddly tangled in one another. Then I looked up at the frost-polished heavens, shuddered in the cold, and finally, closing the window without a sound, eased home the brass bolt on it. Thoughtfully I made my way to bed.

In the morning I woke to find that the frost had painted palm trees on the window-pane. I prepared the Sunday breakfast, then glanced out at the now glittering canvas of the tent. The frost had made the morning air soundless so that the town seemed unusually still. My father always slept out on Sunday mornings. As I came downstairs after having given him his breakfast in bed I heard a low knocking at the side-door.

I tiptoed out into the hallway. As again the knocking came, 'Who's out?' I asked sharply. 'Me!' said the deep hoarse voice which I recognized at once as being that of the bearded tramp. 'What do you want?' I asked. 'A knife—or a scissors,' he growled. I paused, a constriction of fear in my heart. 'My father is in bed,' I told him. 'Can you wait till he gets up?' 'I must get it now—we have to be off!' The man's 'we have to be off' assuaged my latent fear that he meant harm, yet I asked, 'What do you want it for?' 'Something that's caught in the frost!' 'Is it the canvas?' 'Give me a knife or a scissors and I'll return it safely,' he muttered in reply.

I stood irresolute. A knife—no! But I could give him the battered black-and-silver tailor's scissors that was in the drawer of our kitchen table. With a cry of 'Wait!' I ran, rattled open the drawer and, going to the door, opened it cautiously and handed out the scissors. A glimpse told me that the man was sober but his face was haggard and white-cold with traces of drink-rust about his lips. Muttering a word of thanks, he moved away.

After a time, I ran to the scullery, climbed on a chair and, leaning over the sink, looked out on the shelter. What I saw made me cry out and beat with my knuckles on the frame of the window. I unshot the bolt, swung open the window on its hinges and screamed 'No! No!' at the top of my voice.

The tramp, who was kneeling on the ground at one end of the shelter, looked upwards over his shoulder at me. His black hat was pitched back on his poll and a single lock of hair was plastered onto his white sweating forehead. 'No! No!' I screamed again, then leaping off the chair I raced through the kitchen, tore into the shop, grabbed a claw-hammer from the tool-box under the counter and, opening the hall door, went pelting out.

The man, the scissors still in his hands, was on one knee at the end of the tent. Beneath him, prone on the ground and protruding from under the canvas of the shelter, lay the woman's head and breast. The tumult of her hair was spread out beneath her head. I verified what I had guessed at from my first glimpse through the window, that her hair was frostlocked in a small but comparatively deep pool of water that lay just outside the end of the camp and that the tramp was about to cut the hair so as to release it.

The woman's face could have been the one carved in cameo on the brooch my mother wore, but for the fact that the rust of old drink befouled her lips about which an odd not-caring smile now played. The white skin of her lower throat and upper breasts was in startling contrast to her dark complexion and to the soiled ground beneath her head. 'Wait!' I cried again, pushing the man aside; crouching, my fingers verified that the hair was vice-gripped in a frozen pool of animal urine.

I tilted the head sideways and with the hammer-head began to hack at the edge of the frozen pool. Under my blows the ice cracked brown-white at its edges. When I had reduced part of the edge of the pool to powder, I tried with the claw of the hammer to lever upwards on the ragged block of the frozen pool. Try as I would, I failed to gain purchase on the powdered ice.

The man, still in a kind of animal crouch, was directly behind me and watching me dully. He held the scissors in his hand. Again I attacked, seemingly as fruitlessly as before, for even the claw of the hammer could do little more than break off futile smithereens. Although I continued to pound and claw, releasing the hair seemed a baffling task.

I paused; then furious and tense, I snatched the scissors from the man's hand. Forcing its two points together to make a single point, which I thrust deep under the ice-block, I began to lever the ice upwards. At first I made no impression on it but, at last, hearing the ice squeak, I again inserted the scissors at a different place, this time with the points about an inch apart, and, levering with all my strength, brought the whole irregular frozen block in which the spread of the woman's hair was locked, completely free of the ground.

For a moment or two, utterly spent, I hung above the woman; then I half-dragged, half-helped her to her feet where, smiling grotesquely, she continued to regard me sidelong with slightly daft, slightly whimsical, wholly animal eyes. Her neck and shoulders were white and bare and the brown dripping block of ice dangled between her shoulder-blades.

Gripping the hammer and scissors, I began to push her out into the street and towards our hall-door which still stood ajar. I pushed her into the kitchen where by now the morning range was a grin of fire. Sobbing somewhat, I steered her before me into the scullery. There, standing on a chair, I made her bow her neck as I filled an enamel basin with hot water. Cupping the water in my hands, I poured it over the matted poll. I kept working furiously until the melting ice began to fall in chunks into the basin. Then I took up a bar of soap and frenziedly lathered the woman's hair. I found myself working under an odd compulsion.

Not a word passed between us. Again and again I changed the water in the basin until at last, as I rinsed the hair, the water poured clearly. I put a towel about her head and draped a bath-towel over a chair.

I then took out—she watched me dreamily—a large oval-shaped zinc bathtub and, setting it on the floor, affixed a length of hose to the nozzle of the hot-water tap and sent steaming water pouring into the vessel. Almost stamping my foot, I signed to the woman that she should stand in it and wash herself. Dully she began to drop her rags to the floor. I tiptoed upstairs and, opening the mahogany wardrobe on the landing, piled a skirt and blouse of my dead mother over one arm and snatched some underclothes from a drawer beside it. A pair of lizard-skin shoes, old fishnet stockings, these too I took; finally, opening a dusty trunk, I removed a clutch of hairpins and a comb inset with brilliants.

Returning to the kitchen, I peeped through the keyhole into the scullery; the woman was still standing in the steaming tub, indolently rubbing the cake of soap to her limbs. Young as I was, I realized that she had a beautiful body.

I prepared the breakfast. When I thought that she had finished washing herself I pushed open the door a little and left the clothes on the floor inside it. After a time I heard the basin clank against the trough and the scrape of the woman's nails as she rinsed the vessel. A little while later she came slowly out, wearing my mother's clothes.

Holding my breath, I watched her walk forward. The house was without sound. In mid-kitchen she turned and, looking at the table, indicated that she wished to eat. I placed food before her. She ate her breakfast slowly and thoughtfully, crumbs falling unheeded to the floor. When she had finished, I placed the delf on a tray and pointed to the rocking-chair by the fire. The woman rose slowly then went and sat on it. I took the tray to the scullery, piled the ware into a basin, ran the hot water on it and returned to the kitchen. From a press to the left of the fire I took a strong-toothed comb and, standing behind her, unwound the towel turban and set about combing out the drying hair.

I was patient with the hair, teasing it gently where it had knotted and working diligently until at last it was a blue-black thunder-cloud about her head and shoulders. Between me and the glow of the fire its edges were rimmed with red-gold. Wholly absorbed, I kept on combing as the hair became still drier and more beautiful—more tractable too, until at last it glistened and shone and shook and floated and fell in plenitude about her waist. The woman turned her head quite sensitively to accommodate me as I worked.

At last I combed the hair back over the ears and, setting aside the comb, began to plait and pile it, twisting it this way and that, pinning it at a point that took my fancy by inserting the comb with the brilliants in it and then undoing it capriciously as if dissatisfied with the result. The hair, now wholly dry, was sensual under my fingers, so that I was reluctant to finish, and time and again with an exclamation of sham annoyance I let it fall. Each time I broke off, the woman smiled at my feigned disappointment. About us the house grew still more silent.

This went on for some time until I could find no excuse to

continue. Then the woman's long bare arm curled intuitively about me and drew me gently down on to her lap. At first I was inclined to resist, but her implied certainty that I would obey her was so absolute that I yielded. There was a pause in which my buttocks tested the welcome seat offered by her thighs, then, reassured, I sent my arm over her shoulder and dug my fingers deep into the thicket of hair at the nape of her neck.

Almost imperceptibly at first, but with a mounting sense of rhythm, and muttering, humming and crooning as she moved, the woman began to rock backwards and forwards on the chair with a movement reminiscent of the metronome on the piano-top. I found myself nestling closer to her breasts: of its own volition my head butted against her and before I knew, or cared, my lips and teeth were on her nipples. I heard myself, as at a distance, mouthing warm pleasant incoherencies.

So drugged were we both that the vague knocking on the hall door did not disturb us, nor a moment or two later did the sight of my father in the kitchen doorway, dressed only in his pants and shirt, with the bearded tramp standing beside him, trouble us in the least. After an uncomprehending glance at us the two men turned away and moved dully into the bar, leaving us alone to rock out a solution to one of the many compulsions of our shared womanhood.